MW01245082

Small
World

Ronald R Johnson

Copyright © 2017 Ronald R. Johnson

All rights reserved.

ISBN: 1544222246
ISBN-13: 978-1544222240

DEDICATION

To the memory of

Charlotte Runnels

who encouraged me long, long ago

CONTENTS

ACKNOWLEDGMENTS

The cover was designed by Melissa Houtz, using the Earth Rise photo from Apollo 8, courtesy of NASA. I want to thank Connie Moore, Photo Researcher at NASA, for directing me to a high-resolution image of the picture.

Reference is made to the following works:

G. W. F. Hegel, *Elements of the Philosophy of Right*, Allen W. Wood, ed., H. B. Nisbet, trans. (Cambridge: Cambridge University Press, 1991), Preface, p. 20.

"Valley Girl," by Frank Zappa and Moon Unit Zappa, from Frank Zappa's 1982 album *Ship Arriving Too Late to Save a Drowning Witch*.

Francis Thompson, *Hound of Heaven*, John F. Quinn, ed. (Chicago: Loyola University Press, 1970), lines 1-4, 25-29, 178-179.

Deep Throat is based on the character of the same name in Carl Bernstein and Bob Woodward, *All the President's Men* (New York: Warner Books, 1976), pp. 73-75, including the incredible detail about the note on p. 20 of *The New York Times*.

Woody Woodpecker was a cartoon character created by Walter Lantz. He became famous in the 1940s but is still around in 2017 and will probably live to terrorize the Professor for years to come.

I would like to thank my wife Nancy and daughter Emily for their support, which they have each expressed in ways big and small over the years.

1 RUMORS OF MY DEATH

Okay, you win.

I'll start by talking about how I died.

Whether I like it or not, that's what everybody wants to know. "You're not Dak Blayzak," they say. "We saw him die on the Internet."

As a respected journalist, I try to stay out of the stories I'm reporting, but on this one I failed miserably. I should've admitted I was dead right from the start. When you hold back on something like that, people just won't let it go.

You have to understand, though, that I'm touchy on this subject. My critics have long accused me of *making* news rather than reporting it. They quote me as saying, "The point is not to tell the story; it's to change it." For the record, I never said that. I said I want to be wherever big changes are taking place. It's never been my intention to bring about those changes myself.

In this case, however, I admit that my very presence changed everything. But I didn't mean for that to happen. And I certainly didn't plan on dying.

As everyone knows, I was on the moon, in the rugged South Central Highlands, doing an exposé on the Clayborn Clone Community. I had done some pieces on the community's founder, Carl Clayborn, years earlier.

Clayborn's parents were wealthy geeks who wanted to give him a competitive advantage over the *hoi polloi*. Instead of just having a baby the old-fashioned way, they did some genetic engineering, and Carl was born with significant mental endowments. He put those gifts to use immediately, but not in the way they expected. Even as a child, he set out to kill them and inherit their fortune.

1

He didn't succeed, so at the age of eleven he turned to the study of law, and at twelve he took them to court. He argued that their genetic tampering gave them a greater obligation to him than would otherwise have been the case. His superior abilities cried out for full expression—and for that, he needed large sums of money. He won a huge settlement, which he quickly multiplied through clever investments. By the time he reached the age of maturity, he was worth billions.

But it wasn't enough. He didn't just want to be rich. He wanted to rule the world.

Not that he cared about politics—that slow, plodding process that never accomplished anything. He didn't just want to oversee the world; he wanted to rule it with an iron fist.

"In me," he said, "the actual has become rational, and the rational actual." He had borrowed the phrase from the philosopher G. W. F. Hegel, but he felt that Hegel only partially understood it. "He would've cried tears of joy if he had met me," Clayborn liked to say.

Taking advantage of his superior intelligence and abundant resources, Carl Clayborn hatched numerous schemes to bring about world domination. Each one failed, and for the same reason each time: because he couldn't get along with his accomplices. He expected them to recognize him as the supreme leader, but egos always got in the way. As Clayborn saw it, there was only room for one ego. His.

It would take an army to achieve his goals, but he couldn't depend on anyone but himself. The conclusion was obvious. He must create a society of Carl Clayborns: a community of clones.

Cloning himself was no problem, but he needed wombs. He didn't care about their quality. Genes were the thing; the womb was just a temporary housing. So he hired surrogate mothers—"wombs for rent," he called them. He treated the women poorly and paid them little. He didn't even know their names. But when he suddenly had thirty screaming babies on his hands, he realized he needed to keep the women on the job, at least for a while. All of them hated working for Clayborn, but several of them bonded with the infants and tried to give them the love they so desperately needed. A few even tried to teach the kids manners.

Clayborn was horrified. "Slave morality!" he said. "'Pleases' and 'thank yous' will be irrelevant in the society I'm building!"

But he couldn't stop them, because he had problems of his own. By this time, he was wanted for tax evasion and several other crimes, and he kept having to run from the authorities. He took the children with him, but he needed the surrogate mothers to look after them. He gave the women strict childrearing instructions. Some obeyed him; others didn't.

When the boys were twelve years old, he was ready for the next phase of his plan. Over the past several years, he had quietly built a domed village on the moon, where no nation currently had jurisdiction. He fired the surrogate mothers and took his sons with him to his Utopia in the Sky.

That was nine years ago. And now, for no apparent reason, I received an urgent invitation to tour the compound and report on the progress of their community.

I had interviewed Carl a few times throughout his insane career, and we had last met at a secret rendezvous site just before he left on his lunar adventure. I still don't understand exactly why he agreed to talk to me. He wasn't interested in Public Relations. I think he just wanted to brag. He had eluded the authorities of seven countries and was now on his way to a futuristic city-under-glass that he himself had designed and paid for. In the years that followed, there would be many other lunar cities, but his was one of the first, and he was clearly proud of it. He was also proud of his young clones. He called them out from a back room and made them stand at attention.

Thirty young versions of himself, twelve years old, ripe for indoctrination.

I hadn't heard from him in nine years. And now I received this invitation.

My editor, Norton Dodge, said it was a trap.

"Good!" I told him. "I like walking into traps."

"I'm serious."

"So am I. And Naif likes it too, right Naif?"

Naif was my cameraman. His name was pronounced 'Knife,' but don't let that fool you. He was useless in a fight, since he was always holding a lens up to his eye. Chaos could be going on all around him and it wouldn't faze him; the show must go on. He was the best camera guy I ever had, but he went a little overboard. I tried to have a heart-to-heart talk with him once—just once—and I realized he was taping our discussion.

"Put that thing down!" I told him.

He wouldn't do it, so I grabbed it out of his hand. He immediately put his thumb and forefinger together to simulate a lens, and held it up to his eye.

"That's an addiction," I told him. "You should see somebody about that."

But he never did.

I don't mean to say he had a camera strapped to his face at all hours of the day and night. It's just that he reached for it at the slightest

3

provocation.

So now I turned to Naif, who was not taping at the moment. "Dodge says it's a trap. What do you think?"

"I think he's right," Naif said.

"Want to go anyway?"

"Of course! I can't wait to see how those kids turned out."

"They'll all be twenty-one now," I said, and Naif laughed.

"Just waiting to abduct us!"

I nodded. "And use us to take over the world."

"You're both crazy!" Dodge said.

"But it'll make a great story," I replied. "And that's why we're the Number One investigative team on the Internet, right Naif?"

"Take that, Fru Phillips!" he said.

Fru is my nemesis. I have a lot of respect for my other competitors but I've got nothing but contempt for Fru. He sends people to spy on me, and just when I'm about to report breaking news, he shows up. If he had ever demonstrated any initiative of his own, I'd be willing to give him credit, but that guy's a fake. He'd be completely unknown if it wasn't for me. Don't get me started.

Anyway, Naif and I decided we'd better get to the moon before Dodge could stop us. So Maggie, my personal assistant, booked us a flight to Space Station Beta and armed us with phony passports. I was Andrei Popov and Naif was Faisal Kahn.

"Where does she come up with these names?" Naif asked.

"I don't know," I told him, "but Fru will have a tough time trailing us. That's all I care about."

We had no trouble getting past security at the spaceport, and we boarded our flight unrecognized. Of course, my fake moustache and glasses probably helped.

The airbus arrived at Station Beta an hour after liftoff. Once there, we picked up the private shuttle Maggie had reserved for the second leg of our trip. We had no pilot; the shuttle was programmed to take us to our destination. Good thing, because I don't drive, and I certainly don't fly space ships.

2 THE ONE THAT IS MANY

Naif and I had already visited the moon a number of times, especially recently. Increasing numbers of people are moving there these days, and there are lots of good stories developing. It's like the Oregon Trail.

On our first couple of trips, Naif thought the moon lacked visual appeal.

"Everywhere you look, there's gray dust and black sky," he said. "Viewers want color."

But over time, that had changed. Yes, there was still a lot of gray, but there were also pockets of color. A number of pioneer settlements had been established on the moon, and under each of those domes were biospheres mimicking earth's atmosphere: blue skies, green forests, and buildings of various colors. Each trip we took to the moon was more interesting than the previous one, as new settlements were always opening and others were under construction.

The Clayborn Clone Community was situated far from all the others, just as Carl had planned for it to be. He knew where future growth was likely to occur, and he set up camp in an entirely different direction. Although there was a lot of traffic when we left Station Beta and headed toward the moon, all other vehicles had broken away from us hours ago. Clayborn had sensors watching for intruders, and he probably knew we were coming long before we got there. Nobody else ever went where we were going.

At last the shuttle made its descent, and Naif started taping.

The compound looked like a little town under glass. Inside were rolling hills, a farm, a library, a residence hall, a lake, tennis courts, a space observatory, and an open-air theater.

As our shuttle approached, a computerized voice demanded to know who we were and why we were there.

"I'm Dak Blayzak from the Global News Network."

"Visitors are not welcome."

"I have an invitation. I'll send it to you."

I did so.

"This is not official," the computer voice told me.

"That's your problem, not mine. Someone from inside sent it to me. Do you deny that?"

No answer.

"Hello? Can you confirm or deny that someone from your community sent me that message?"

There was a long pause, and then the voice said, "You will proceed to Entrance A-1. Your craft will be piloted remotely. When it has landed, you will await further orders."

"I'm not too good at following orders."

The entrance was a pressurized glass tunnel. We sat inside it for so long, Naif and I wondered if they were ever going to let us all the way in. Finally our shuttle lurched forward and we were inside the dome. We flew over a spaceport and an adjacent hangar filled with one-man space pods.

After hovering a moment, we came to rest on the landing pad.

The door of our shuttle was opened by the computer, and a wheeled rectangular robot, about five feet tall, came up the ramp. "You will follow me. Do not deviate from the path." It pointed a ray gun at us.

"Very subtle," I said. "You ready, Naif?"

"Always."

"Okay. Show time."

The main building was a short walk from our shuttle. It was architecturally unique, with a style unlike any on earth. Leave it to Clayborn not to borrow from previous architects; he probably considered their work inferior to his.

As we crossed the courtyard, we could hear voices whispering from all directions.

I looked around this way and that. Naif did the same thing with his video camera. But there was no one in sight.

We approached the main building but were not allowed to go through the front entrance. Instead, we passed through a back door that was incredibly narrow. It seemed to have been built for robots, not people.

Once inside, our guide led us down a long, curved corridor. The walls were lavender, with quotations in numerous languages strung along them. I couldn't read any of the quotes, but I was sure that all the residents could.

Watching the robot gliding ahead of us, I got an idea. I texted Naif a message and he nodded.

"I'll tell you when," I said.

The corridor opened onto a large vestibule. It had a glass ceiling, and sunlight streamed in. There were paintings and sculptures which I had never seen before but which seemed as good as any I had ever seen in the world's art museums. I assumed that they had been produced by Clayborn's offspring.

Naif and I tried to take it all in, but the robot warned us to keep up.

We entered a narrow hallway so dark that I couldn't even see our guide. Fortunately, the robot made a humming sound, so I just followed that.

The hallway emptied out into a circular room. I couldn't believe what I was seeing.

I turned to our guide. "A chapel?"

A soft blue light illuminated everything. Thirty chairs were arranged in a circle, each one reclined backwards to draw the eye upward. There, in the ceiling, was an aperture, and within its center was the earth, floating in space. Around the opening was the inscription: "One day... this will be yours." We were not permitted to sit in these chairs; we were left standing in the center of the room, waiting.

From the moment we entered the sanctuary, I heard a strange sound that I could not at first identify. It came from everywhere, and it was like a gentle breeze, but when it increased in volume, I realized that it was a chorus of male voices. Scores of young men in blue robes stepped out from the shadows of the room, singing a song without lyrics—an otherworldly succession of complex chords, sliding almost imperceptibly between dissonance and resolution, dissonance and resolution. Then they began to sing words. Although there was still no recognizable melody, the song now took on a hopeful tone, and there was a kind of question-response interplay among the voices:

> *In us...*
> *(In uuuuussss...)*
> *The Rational...*
> *(Rash-un-uuuuuullll...)*
> *Has become Actual...*
> *(Ack-shoooo-uuuuuulllll...)*
> *And the Actual...*

7

Has become Rational...
(Rash-un-uuuuuullll...)

Now the voices sounded jubilant as they sang, at last, in a conventional melodic structure:

We are The One That Is Many...
The Many That Are One!

Then came the wordless conclusion, which sounded suspiciously like the Sevenfold Amen. When the last chord faded, the young singers filed out of the room without a word.

This was our only chance.

"Now!" I told Naif, and we both slammed into the robot, knocking it on its left side. The flap to the ray gun was pinned down, and the box-shaped robot was unable to get back up on its wheels.

"You will stop!" it said, almost pleadingly. "You will go no farther!"

Motioning to Naif, I hurried after the retreating clones. We reached the vestibule in time to see the young men escaping through several doorways at once. Just as we were about to overtake the last of them, I noticed an emaciated old man in a hoverchair just inside one of the doors. It was Carl Clayborn, and there were tears streaming down his face.

"Help me!" he said, extending his hand in my direction. "Save me!"

But before I could get near enough to speak, all the doors slid shut and everyone was gone.

Three rectangular robots appeared from adjoining hallways and surrounded us, aiming guns at us. "You have abused our hospitality. You are now our prisoners."

3 BE OUR GUEST

I'm not sure how many hours passed. We were locked in a small, plain room with a bunk bed and a tiny adjacent bathroom. It wasn't a bad place, considering we were under arrest. To our surprise, we had Internet access and could call for help if we wanted to do so, but we decided to wait it out. We had a story to cover, and we didn't want to leave until we were finished.

At one point, I was pacing and thinking while Naif had his eyes closed on the bottom bed. (That was the one time when Naif could be sure to set his camera aside, by the way. He didn't sleep with his camera, in case you were wondering.)

Suddenly we heard chimes.

Naif opened one eye. "What was that?"

They played again. This time I recognized the melody: it was the Clayborn Theme Song we had heard in the chapel earlier: "The One That Is Many."

"Sounds like a doorbell," Naif said.

"In a jail cell?" But I found a button near the door and pushed it. One of the clones entered quickly, shutting the door behind him.

"We have only a moment," he told us. "I disabled the cameras, but it won't take the others long to discover the problem and fix it."

Naif and I looked around the room. "*What* cameras?"

"You must listen carefully," he said. "Your lives are in danger as long as you stay here. I have arranged to smuggle you out—on one condition. I'm coming with you."

"We just got here," I said.

Naif reached for his camera and started taping. The clone turned away from him nervously. "Make him stop," he pleaded. "They'll kill me if

9

they find out."

I signaled for Naif to put the camera away, and the clone relaxed slightly.

"*Who* will kill you?" I asked.

The chimes rang again.

"It's them!" he said. "I'm doomed!"

The kid's eyes searched the room frantically, then he dived under the bed.

Naif and I looked at each other. I pushed the button and another clone stepped in, closing the door behind him.

"We don't have much time," he said. "I disabled the cameras, but someone will fix them in a matter of minutes."

Naif smirked at me.

"You're not safe here," the clone said. "I'm going to help you escape, but only if you take me with you."

I frowned. "Why do you want to leave?"

"Why wouldn't I? Life is so dreary here," he moaned, "and everybody's so ugly."

Naif cleared his throat. "But doesn't that make *you*—?"

The chimes rang again.

The kid started to scramble under the bed before I could warn him. Then he stopped and whispered, "Blackey?"

"Be quiet and get in," said the first clone. "You want us both killed?"

"Aw, they won't kill us. They'll rough us up, maybe, but—"

"Just climb in and keep quiet!"

I pushed the button and another clone entered. This time I shut the door myself.

"We have to be quick about this," the boy said.

"Why?" I asked. "You disabled the cameras, didn't you?"

He stared at me. "Yes, but—"

"But it won't be long until someone finds out, is that it?"

The kid was at a loss for words. "Uh—"

"What do you say, Naif? It would sure be nice if someone would help us escape from this place, don't you think?"

"I can do that," the kid said eagerly, "but only on one condition."

"Right. Join the crowd."

"Huh?"

Two heads stuck out from under the bed. "Smiley!" the first clone said. "Do you wanna get us all killed?"

The latest clone was stunned. "Blackey! Gabby! What are you guys doing here?"

"Having a slumber party. What do you *think* we're doing?"

The chimes rang again.

"Any room under there, guys?" Smiley asked.

"Just be quiet and climb in."

I pushed the button and another clone entered. This one was bald.

Neither of us had a chance to say anything before the voices under the bed cried out, "Good lord, Harry! Get in here and shut that door behind you!"

Harry looked around, confused. "Blackey? Gabby?"

"Keep your voice down," said Blackey. "Do you want to get us all killed?"

He stumbled in and I shut the door.

"Hi, Harry," said another voice.

"Smiley? Where are you guys?"

"Under here."

He crouched down and shook his head in disbelief. "What are you doing under there?"

Naif butted in. "The real question is, How many more of you will fit?"

Harry rubbed his jaw. "Are you here for the same reason I am?"

"That depends," replied Gabby. "Are you sick of seeing your own face looking back at you?"

"I'm sick of everything," Harry said. "The food, the regimentation, the song..."

Everybody groaned. "The song! Every day! Can't we sing something else once in a while?"

"Hey!" Smiley protested. "I wrote that song! And it would sound a lot better if Gabby would stay in tune."

Gabby looked confused. "What are you talking about?"

"You don't even realize it. 'Ack-shoo-UUUULLLL. Rash-shun-UUULLLL.' Right there, you go flat every time."

"I do not!"

Blackey nodded. "It's true. It nearly drives me crazy."

"I'm afraid I have to agree," said Harry. "I'd say you were tone-deaf, Gabby, but we share the same genetic makeup."

All the clones laughed except Gabby.

"I never knew anybody else felt the same way I did about that," said Smiley. "I always thought I was alone."

Harry nodded. "I've never felt free to criticize anything around here. I didn't think anyone would be receptive." He paused a moment. "It's kind of nice."

There was an embarrassed silence, then Gabby broke in. "I do not go flat!"

The chimes rang again and everybody froze.

"I'll hide in the bathroom," Harry offered.

I pushed the button and another clone invited himself in. He ran around the room nervously, looking for something.

"Can I help you?" I asked.

"I'm looking for the cameras. I'm sure there must be some."

"What?" I said. "Didn't you disable them first?"

He shrugged. "I don't know how."

"But he makes an amazing cheese soufflé," said a voice from under the bed. Everybody laughed.

Harry stepped out of the bathroom. "Cook?"

"Harry! What's going on?"

Harry shrugged. "Apparently great minds really do think alike."

4 CLONE CONFAB

So now we had quite a little party going. The boys were enjoying themselves so much, they lost track of time. This was the first chance they had ever had to air their grievances.

They talked about the song again.

"Can't we jazz it up a little?" someone asked. "I've been working on a Big Band arrangement."

Smiley was indignant. "It's meant to be worshipful. If you jazz it up, you'll ruin it."

Another clone interrupted. "Liturgy is for people, not people for liturgy. I say let's jazz it up."

But then they moved onto other subjects, like their desire to escape from the community.

"It's really the Old Man's fault," someone said.

"Oh, wake up. He doesn't make the rules."

"Not anymore. But he started the whole thing."

"He was naïve, that's all. He didn't realize there would be power struggles among his children."

"I disagree," said another. "I think he intended for us to battle it out. He just didn't realize they'd turn on him, too."

Then they began to talk somewhat cryptically about one clone in particular whom they all feared, but they avoided saying his name.

"Things have settled down now that he's eliminated his rivals."

"He killed *them*," said Blackey. "He'll kill us, too."

"Technically, he didn't kill them. He put them in an ingenious trap and they killed themselves by trying to break out. They'd be alive today if they had had more patience."

"But they hadn't been fed in days. How much patience can a man have?"

My curiosity got the better of me. "Who are you talking about?"

They were all silent a moment, then Harry answered. "His name's Clarence, but he calls himself 'The One.'"

Everybody looked disgusted.

"It's a travesty!" said Blackey. "A desecration!"

Gabby explained. "We're *all* 'The One,' you see. We're 'The One That Is Many, The Many That Are One.' That's our community identity. For any individual to claim that HE is the ONE AND ONLY One is like spitting on all of us."

"And he gets away with it through fear and intimidation."

"And murder," Blackey added.

Cook looked thoughtful. "Sometimes I used to think the Old Man considered *himself* 'The One.'"

Others nodded. "The way he talked sometimes, I, too, got the impression that he thought of himself as 'The One' from which 'The Many' sprang. But that's not the concept I grew up having."

Enthusiasm spread around the room. "Exactly! Sometimes it was an almost mystical experience picturing myself as part of something bigger than me. Each of us is connected to each... and to all!"

"I've felt more than just elation," said Smiley. "I've had a profound sense of responsibility. As we sing my song and look up at the earth—so beautiful, so vulnerable—I want to cradle it in my arms."

Harry nodded. "I've always imagined us going back there... spreading out... all over the globe... and using our superior intelligence to care for the world."

"I've thought that, too!" said Gabby. "I believe it's our destiny to use our skills in the service of mankind. And no matter what happens, from this day forward, we'll have each other. We'll always be One."

Silence fell over the group as they pondered that thought.

Without chimes or any other warning, the door opened and a powerful-looking clone entered, flanked by two other clones.

"It's him!" the group whispered.

He stood there a moment, then turned to his henchmen. "Lefty... Righty... clear the room."

Like an explosion, the group blasted out the door *en masse*, leaving The One and his henchmen alone with Naif and me. Naif grabbed his video camera.

The One approached me and looked me over, but he spoke to his henchmen rather than to me. "They're a disease," he said. "They've infected our culture. I tried to quarantine them, but it wasn't enough."

"Should we kill them now?" asked Lefty.

He considered that suggestion, then shook his head. "No... not yet."

He circled me again, thought a moment, then left the room with a martial step, his henchmen following close behind.

It had been a long day, and Naif and I decided to get some sleep. But as I climbed into the top bunk, I heard a signal from my phone. It was a message from Deep Throat.

Deep Throat was the best informant a journalist could have. I had never met him, and I wasn't sure who he was, but he had helped me on many occasions, providing invaluable guidance. He only gave me information on "deep background," meaning I could never quote him, not even anonymously, but his advice was always helpful and his information was always completely accurate. To know the things he knew, he must have been highly placed in government circles. I would've loved to meet him face-to-face, but we had an understanding. When he had information, he would leave a message on page twenty of my digital *New York Times*. I had no idea how he got access to my paper, but I was always glad to hear from my friend, and I programmed my phone to ding me whenever there was a message.

Here's what he had for me today:

> *Forget the clones. A better story is breaking on the far side of the moon. Here are the coordinates.*

I stared blankly at the screen for a moment. He knew where I was. Surely he also knew that I was being held captive, yet he was urging me to leave. It didn't make sense. But when I thought about it, I realized that Deep Throat was never wrong. So I sent the coordinates to our shuttle and instructed it to be ready to take us there as soon as I boarded. The shuttle responded affirmatively. Then I drifted off to sleep.

5 A LOT OF FUSS OVER A LITTLE PILL

The next morning I found an attractive e-card waiting in my email inbox.

"Naif, look at this!"

It was from the clones. "We had a lovely evening," they said, and they added their electronic signatures.

"A thank you card!" said Naif, taping. "Somebody raised those kids right."

I nodded. "Their surrogate mothers did. Or some of them, anyway."

There was a postscript telling us that they had spent the night gauging the moods of others in the community, and there were even more clones who wanted to leave. They also attached a long letter, catching us up on what had been happening in the community the past nine years. It was a frightening chronicle of power struggles, of various subgroups trying to intimidate individuals to join them, of brainwashing and even torture, and yet of the resourcefulness of each individual who found ways to resist.

"I can't believe what those boys have been through," Naif said, still taping.

"And survived," I added. "They don't seem the least bit disillusioned."

I was particularly struck by the lessons Carl had tried to teach them. I knew he had formed secret organizations in the days before making the clones, but one group in particular had continued on without him. They called themselves "The Kindred," and over the years they had gained key spots in all major governments. Carl was proud of them, even though they had betrayed him, and he kept tabs on them through the Internet. In recent years the in-fighting had become especially nasty, and many members of the organization seemed to be losing hope. Carl told the clones the time might be ripe for them to return and take over the organization.

I turned to Naif. "Have you ever heard of this group?"

He shook his head. "I guess that's why they call it a secret."

I kept reading. The boys said they were forced to do daily drills, fending off attacks from robots armed with laser guns and other weapons.

"Aerobics with a purpose," said Naif.

The door opened and three clones rushed in.

"Dak!" said the first. "We've got to move quickly. The One has made his decision. He wants you dead, but he's got to make it look like an accident."

"Right!" said the second. "And there's only one way to keep him from killing you."

The third nodded. "We've got to convince him that the accident has already happened."

Naif and I looked at each other warily. "How are you planning to do that?"

The first clone held up a little pill.

"Now wait a minute," I said. "You want me to swallow the Juliet?"

Like the potion used by its famous namesake, the Juliet is a pill that puts a person into a comatose state almost indistinguishable from death.

"I don't want to die," I said, "even if it's only temporary."

The three of them started toward me.

"Naif?"

I turned toward him, but of course he was taping.

I wanted nothing to do with it. Aside from the fact that you feel exactly like you're dying, there are other drawbacks, like the possibility that people will think you really are dead, throw you in a hole, and cover you with dirt.

I remembered the case of Cochran Hull. He took the Juliet to escape execution. It worked, but he regained consciousness during his own autopsy. Fortunately for him, he lived for less than a minute—just long enough to see some of his organs in plastic containers.

"Nope," I said. "No deal."

The three of them tried to force me to take the pill. "Cook made it. He's also a chemist, you know."

I balked. I don't know chemistry, but I've heard that an inexact measurement could kill a person for real.

"Don't worry," they said. "We have superior intelligence, remember? Besides, Cook added a little jalapeno to give it a festive flair."

I refused, so they held me tight and stuffed it in my mouth. I spit it across the room.

"We'll hold him," two of them said. "You go get it, Gimpy."

Ka-BOOM ka-BOOM ka-BOOM ka-BOOM.

He picked it up and blew on it. "Ten Second Rule," he said. Then he ran back.

Ka-BOOM ka-BOOM ka-BOOM ka-BOOM.

They jammed it back in my mouth. I spit it across the room a second time.

"Would you cut that out!" they said.

Gimpy sighed and went after it again.

Soon it was back in my mouth. They were pinching my lips shut and stroking my throat when The One and his henchmen entered the room.

All four of us gulped in unison.

"So it's true!" said The One. "They made a death pill and forced him to swallow it. What a bunch of geniuses. Lefty... Righty... induce vomiting!"

The clones stood between me and the thugs. With a flourish, they pulled clean, white gloves out of their pockets.

"You wouldn't dare," Lefty said.

Two of the clones stepped forward and lightly slapped the thugs' cheeks with their gloves. That was all it took. The four combatants hurried out to the vestibule and donned their fencing gear. The duel was on.

6 SIBLING RIVALRY

Gimpy led me out to the action and urged me to stay out of the way. Naif was busy taping.

Suddenly, clones appeared from all adjoining hallways. They were already suited up in fencing gear, each one sparring with an opponent. The sound of clashing foils filled the hall.

Into this bedlam came Carl Clayborn on his hoverchair. At the sight of him, everyone stopped.

He was beaming. "Boys! Boys!" he said. "I have an announcement to make. Come closer."

The clones took off their fencing helmets and formed a circle around the Old Man.

He appeared about ready to burst. "You know, of course, that I was genetically engineered—that I was born far superior to other humans. You also know that you are exact replications of me—that you are superior in exactly the ways in which I am superior."

The clones nodded and looked around at each other, their curiosity building.

"What you don't know is that, when I was creating you, I had a brief lapse of self-indulgence." He paused to chuckle. "My *intellectual* gifts were quite sufficient to pass on to you, but I always wondered what I might have been like with certain physical enhancements. I decided to try a little experiment... just once. His intelligence... well... there were complications... but his body! That turned out magnificently! I've been hiding him from you, but now his time has come."

The clones looked worried.

The Old Man could not contain himself. "Boys," he said, "meet Sumo Carl!"

A door slid open and a massive version of the clones came flying out at high speed. His face was similar to theirs, but he was monstrous, and all muscle. He wore only a loin cloth.

Lefty and Righty hurried forward to stop him. With a single effortless move, he knocked their heads together and dropped them on the floor, unconscious. All the other clones stepped aside, and Sumo Carl headed straight for The One. He tried to flee, but the big guy picked him up and held him over his head.

The One shouted, "Computer! Activate 'End Game'!"

Sumo Carl dropped him as robots of various sizes and shapes rushed in from all corridors and began shooting ray guns. In an instant, all the remaining clones joined together as one. Some pulled out a metal device that resembled a catcher's mitt. Jumping and diving, they caught the death rays that were ricocheting around the room. Others had what looked like TV remotes; they made the robots incapable of emitting rays. Almost as suddenly as the commotion had begun, it stopped. Then all the clones turned toward The One.

"Computer!" he said. "Activate 'Plan B'!"

Each robot now produced a circular saw and began chasing the clones. I didn't know the Old Man's hoverchair could fly that fast. Even Sumo Carl ran for his life.

After a moment's confusion, several of the clones began wielding thick clubs. They leaped and whirled around the robots in a graceful dance, now smashing a metallic arm off, now knocking a robot on its side, now bending one's arm so that it sawed itself in two. Somebody handed Sumo Carl a club and he put it to good use, sending robots flying in all directions. Within minutes, all of them were disarmed.

Still holding their clubs, the clones surrounded The One and shouted in unison:

> *We are The One That Is Many...*
> *The Many That Are One!*

"Listen, boys," he said nervously. "You don't want to injure me. We're all One, remember?"

They considered his words carefully, and one-by-one they dropped their weapons. Then they leaped on him and started pounding him with their fists.

While this was happening, doors opened and some familiar faces flooded the vestibule.

I turned to Naif. "Can you believe this?"

He kept filming, but he laughed and shook his head.

It was The Cavalry. Or at least that's what Naif and I called them. They always showed up when we needed them most. It never seemed to matter where we were. When we got in too deep, The Cavalry came in to save us. We didn't know who they were, but we assumed they were government agents. We called their leader 'The Guy' because we didn't know his name.

The Cavalry got down to work pulling the boys off each other, and The Guy came over to me.

"You okay, Dak?"

I opened my mouth to answer him, and then it happened. Without a word, I fell to the ground—dead.

Naif was too busy filming the action to notice. The camera picked it up, but only in the corner of the screen. That's what made viewers suspicious: they could see me clutching my heart and falling to the ground, but nobody explained what was happening. And when the camera panned away to zero in on the clones, viewers got the impression that they weren't meant to see it. To complicate matters, Naif submitted the piece with his own commentary, since I wasn't around to narrate afterwards. That made viewers even more wary.

A lot happened in the next several minutes. A few of the clones put me on a stretcher and carried me to my shuttle. After making sure that I was comfortable, they hurried back to join the others. The Cavalry was sorting out the good guys from the bad—no easy task in a crowd of clones—and the Old Man was telling them how proud he was of them.

"This is the day I've waited for," he said, fighting back tears. "You've passed the test. Now let's oust these interlopers and prepare to rule the world!"

The Guy pushed a button on the back of the Old Man's hoverchair and it dropped to the ground, immobilized. The clones all laughed. Then they went around doing a strange sort of handshake in which they gripped each other's upper arm. As each one reached out to a buddy with his right, he was grasped by another on his left. They went around the group so that each one greeted all the others. "The One That is Many," they murmured again and again as they passed down the line. "The Many That Are One."

"Hey," Naif said, lowering his camera. "Anybody seen Dak?"

A few of the clones escorted Naif out to the courtyard just in time to see my shuttle as a tiny dot, flying away in the distance. Then Naif remembered: last night I had given the shuttle the coordinates I had received from Deep Throat, and I had told it to take off as soon as I boarded. In obedience to those instructions, the shuttle was now carrying my lifeless body to the far side of the moon.

7 AN UNINVITED VISITOR

Very few people have property on the moon's far side. It takes a special kind of person to want to live there, because you can't see the earth. Land is cheap, but there's not a lot of interest.

The shuttle flew to a spot far from any human habitation and came to rest outside a single prefab cabin. The man who lived there had to wear a spacesuit if he ventured out, and he had done that only once since his arrival two months earlier. But after some hesitation, he put on his suit and approached my shuttle.

The outer door opened, letting him into the initial entryway. Once that door closed and the entryway had become pressurized, the inner door opened. He let himself in.

The lights were off, and at first he couldn't find a living soul on board. He took off his space suit and tried to figure out what to do. Then he noticed my lifeless body...

Waking up from the Juliet Trance is like being propelled at high speed through a tunnel, face first. Most people come out of it screaming. I gave more of a shout.

I opened my eyes, but everything was blurry. I was in my shuttle—I could tell that much—but it wasn't moving. It was on the ground. And the lights were off.

I was sweating. My mouth was dry, head spinning.

"Naif?"

There was no answer, and yet I sensed I was not alone.

"Hello?"

Someone moved toward me.

"Who is it?"

In the darkness, I could see the outline of a man.

A man with a gun.

I strained my eyes to see, but he was in the shadows. Then he took another step forward.

As soon as I saw his face, I knew I had interviewed him once. Who was he? My mind was cloudy, but I forced myself to think.

"Insanity is a gift..."

I could hear the gunman saying it. He spoke with a fake British accent. He said "shhedule" instead of "schedule." I remembered that much about him, and those words:

"Insanity is a gift..."

Yes... he had said that on camera. What was the rest of the sentence?

Then I remembered the interview... or that part of it, at least.

"I almost went insane once," he had told me. "Unfortunately, it didn't last."

My disgust must have shown, because he had looked at me impatiently.

"You think it's a curse to go insane, I suppose. You're mistaken. It's a gift from the gods. All the great thinkers of the past were madmen." He appeared lost in thought for a moment, and then he added, "Madness is the only appropriate response to the postmodern world."

Naif had slowly zoomed in on his face, as if to let our viewers see what a madman looked like up close.

Trying to hold my spinning head steady, I now said to the man with the gun, "You... you're that professor."

"Then you do remember," he said quietly.

"Yes," I told him. "It's coming back slowly."

He was a linguist. He had spent his life studying a language that no longer existed. It had been forgotten even by scholars—until now. He spent much of his career reconstructing it.

"Nobody cares," I told him.

Now I could see *that* part of the interview vividly. I always like to rattle my guests. They're supposed to rise to the challenge, but in that moment I could see he didn't know how. He looked shocked, as if I had reached over and slapped him in the face.

"What's the point?" I had said on camera. "Why study a language that nobody in the world uses?"

His face turned bright red. "I don't even know how to answer that," he said.

Naif let the camera rest on his face as we sat there in silence, but I was thinking, *If you can't speak in defense of your own life's work, then how do you expect anyone else to understand?*

One of my education sources had suggested I do a piece on him. The Professor had been kicked out of Harvard because he wouldn't play by the rules. Under the old tenure system he would've been untouchable, but times had changed and the Professor had few friends among the faculty. His ousting hadn't provoked much of a scandal, but it was still somewhat unusual. I interviewed him to see what it was all about.

His colleagues at other Ivy League schools all spoke well of him. They said he had done something incredible in his field. But students hated him. He was boring, pompous, thin-skinned, and had no sympathy for them. They said his grading patterns were unpredictable. They petitioned the Dean, who investigated and discovered the Professor on the verge of a nervous breakdown.

"Your grades are overdue," the Dean said.

The Professor shrugged. "Give them all F's."

"We can't do that!"

"Give them all A's, then. What do I care?"

So the Professor was shown the door. I interviewed him shortly afterwards. Some of his friends were hoping that he'd acquit himself publicly and perhaps build on that to get another teaching job, but we didn't get far into the interview before I knew better. This man was a mess. I even handed him a couple of simple questions and he treated me like I was stupid. The end result was a freak show.

After we ran the interview, he left a message on my video mail. He was opposed to leaving such messages, he said, but it was his only alternative. He strongly protested the way we had edited the piece. He accused me of chopping up our conversation into tiny bite-sized platitudes which no longer remotely resembled what he had said.

"Human intelligence is an organic whole—if and when it is exercised, and in your case I'm sure it is seldom. If you ask a thinking man a question and he gives you an answer out of the depths of his soul, you must take what he says in its fullness. You can't cut pieces out of it without doing damage to the entire thought. The pieces by themselves mean nothing."

Well, maybe so, but that's the way a journalistic interview works. If a person doesn't want to play by those rules, he shouldn't agree to be interviewed.

I concede that an edited interview is only an incomplete report of a much larger discussion, but I do not agree that a shortened version can't do justice to the original. The key to good editing is to interpret the original interview in a fair and balanced way. If the journalist understands what the subject was trying to say, he's justified in cutting the interview to make it fit the time constraints. I understood the Professor perfectly well. I just wasn't sympathetic. And I guess that came across on the screen.

I'm not sorry about anything we put in that report. Every word of it was true, and nothing was taken out of context. I admit that Naif shot a lot of close-ups of the Professor's long fingernails, especially when he used them to clean out his ears while he was talking. He also did a brilliant 360-degree pan around the Professor's head to show his unique haircut (apparently the Professor liked to put a bowl over his head and snip away with scissors at anything that stuck out the bottom). But that was just good camera work that helped convey an image of the man.

A month or two before Naif and I visited the moon, I learned that the Professor had gone there himself—to the far side, to live as a hermit. He would never have to look upon the earth again, for the far side of the moon always faces away from Planet Earth. I felt a twinge of guilt when I heard the news, and I wondered if I was part of the reason he had turned his back on the human race.

But now I was alone with him, and he was holding a gun on me.

8 THE PROFESSOR AND THE BURLAP SACK

I glanced at the gun momentarily and looked away—then I stared at it. "Where did you get that?" I asked.

He seemed surprised by the question and pointed the gun at his own face. "What—*this?*"

"It must be a couple hundred years old!"

"What does that matter?" he asked.

"Does it even work?"

"I can assure you it is quite deadly."

"Care to bet on that?"

"Now listen, you," he said. "Show some respect or I'll—" The sentence hung unfinished for a long, embarrassing moment.

"Is that what this is about?" I asked. "Respect?"

He was going to ask me what I meant, but then he stopped, nodded, and grimaced. "I see. You think I'm here to settle an old score."

"Aren't you?"

He puckered his lips angrily. "You must think I'm some sort of crackpot."

I didn't answer immediately. "You've entered my shuttle uninvited," I finally said, "and you're holding me at gunpoint. I guess I don't know what else to think."

He looked at the pistol a moment and, with a sigh, placed it on the table between us. "I couldn't have shot you anyway. It would've ruined everything."

"Damn right," I said, picking up the weapon. "This is a pressurized cabin. Do you know what would happen if a stray bullet hit one of the walls?"

He shrugged. "I've never cared about technology."

"Well, if you're going to live alone on the moon, you'd better start caring or someday you might do something stupid."

He bristled and seemed to be searching for an appropriate comeback, but gave up.

I opened the revolver. "Hey, you didn't even load it!"

He shrugged again. "I told you… it would've ruined everything if I had gone through with it."

I gave him back the gun. "What's this all about?"

He inhaled quickly like I had just ripped a bandage off a wound; then he exhaled slowly, hissing through his teeth. I expected him to answer me when the hissing stopped, but instead he inhaled and exhaled all over again. Finally, I broke in. "Professor!"

"All right, all right," he said. "You'll ridicule me—but I have to tell you."

"Tell me what?"

He inhaled again. "I have discovered proof that we are not alone in the universe."

Oh brother.

"What kind of proof?" I asked.

"I have received a message from an alien race."

"And you want me to relay this message to the public, is that it?"

"No," he answered crisply. "That's not it."

"What a relief."

"Your celebrity status means nothing to these aliens, nor does it mean anything to me."

"Then what do you want?"

He looked at me hard, the corner of his mouth forming a malevolent grin. "The earth and all its inhabitants will be destroyed in ten days unless we do what the aliens have commanded."

"We?" I asked.

"You and me."

This made no sense whatsoever. "And what are—we—supposed to do?"

"There is an extra-terrestrial living on earth right now. No one knows that he's an alien. You and I have ten days to find him. If we succeed, the human race will be spared. If we fail—"

"Okay, I get the picture. Where are we supposed to look?"

"He could be anywhere on earth."

"Super. Do we know anything about him?"

"His name is Basil."

I bit my lip. "An alien named Basil. Okay… any last name?"

He shook his head.

"So," I said, "you and I have until—" I thought a moment "—until the 24th to find somebody named Basil. No last name. No description. Could be anywhere. If we don't find him, we're all toast. Anything else I should know?"

"Yes," he said, watching my reaction carefully. "One more thing."

I waited, but he just kept watching me. Then he walked to the corner of the room and picked up a burlap sack.

"Where do you find this stuff?" I asked. "Who has burlap anymore?"

Bringing the bag back to his seat, he pulled out a metallic object, tubular in shape, about two feet long and an inch or so in diameter. On its face was a screen like the old LED monitors of the late twentieth century. At each end was a kind of handlebar. It looked like a metal rolling pin.

Reverently, the Professor began to pass it over to me.

"What is it?" I asked, reluctant to take it.

He stopped, placed it in his lap, and sat back. "It is a communicator. This is how the aliens have transmitted their thoughts to me. It was buried not far from here, probably several thousand years ago. I uncovered it earlier today."

"And how did you find it?"

He smiled. "This was the final chapter of a drama that has been unfolding for most of my life. My research—what did you call it on your program? Arcane?"

Esoteric. But there was no point in quibbling.

"My 'arcane' research led me to the discovery that aliens had visited the earth, somewhere in the Fertile Crescent, several thousand years ago."

I sighed impatiently. "This is an old, boring story."

"That's what I thought at first," he said, "until I discovered fragments from an ancient Sumerian text telling about an encounter with an alien. Naturally, the author of the text referred to him as a divine being, but it is quite clear that the visitor was merely an alien from another planet. The text said that there would be another visitation again someday, when men had begun to populate the moon. I found all of this mildly interesting, of course, but I was quite taken aback when I read a passage that described, in detail and with complete accuracy, the place where I have been staying here on the moon's far side."

"How can that be?" I asked. "This side of the moon is never visible from the earth."

"Exactly," he replied. "That was what impressed me. So I went to the place that was described in the text, and I found this."

He handed the Communicator to me.

"Hold on to each end," he said, "and watch what happens."

I thought about it for a moment, and then I gave in. As soon as I gripped the instrument with both hands, hieroglyphs appeared on the screen.

9 UNCLE WOODY

"What the—" I said, backing away from it.

"I will accept that as an apology," he said triumphantly. "You really did think I was making it all up, didn't you?"

"So you're telling me that… when I grabbed onto that thing… it was like I had picked up a hotline to somebody Out There, and those hieroglyphs were their way of saying hello?"

"Something like that," he said. "Remember, their original communication with humans was carried out in an extinct Sumerian tongue. Naturally, they think we still speak that language. So, to accommodate us, they're communicating in those ancient symbols."

I processed this information. "What were they trying to say to me?"

"I was unable to read it," he said, "but if your case is anything like mine, I presume they were offering you a clue about how to find Basil."

I took a deep breath. "I'm all for that. Let's try it again."

Once more, I held onto both ends of the metallic bar. This time the Professor looked at it, mumbled something, and returned to his seat.

"What is it?" I asked.

He stroked his chin. "It would appear that things are going to be a bit more complicated than I had supposed."

After a moment more of silence, I pressed for an explanation.

He sighed. "I had thought that you and I were to search for Basil alone. At first I had believed, perhaps naively, that the aliens had chosen me—only me—to save the human race. When they mentioned you, I was quite surprised."

"I've been wondering about that," I said. "Why me?"

"Yes… 'why you' indeed. But try as I might to persuade the aliens that you and I could never work together, they insisted that I contact you."

"So you packed up your gun and came looking for me."

He shook his head. "I never had to do that. You came to me. I don't understand why."

"I'll explain later," I told him. "At any rate, now you've found me. So what did the Communicator say to me just now?"

The Professor looked crestfallen. "Apparently you and I are not going to find Basil by ourselves. When you held the Communicator, it told you the name of a person whom you must contact."

"What for?" I asked.

"It's not entirely clear, but I assume that, at some point, this procedure is going to lead us to Basil."

"You assume…"

"Yes," he said. "Evidently that's the plan."

I sighed. "Okay. Who do they want me to contact?"

"Let me see it again," he said.

I held the handlebars of the Communicator, and the message appeared again on the screen.

"There are two characters," he told me. "The first refers to one of your kinsmen of the generation just preceding yours. An uncle, I believe."

"All right," I said. "That should be easy. I don't have many uncles."

"The second character is difficult to translate. It is adjectival in its suffix but seems to refer to a fibrous material of some kind. A wood-like substance. 'Woody,' I suppose would be the proper translation." He thought about it a moment and then said, "I believe they're trying to tell you to contact your Uncle Woody."

We looked at each other for a moment. "Well, that'll be hard," I said, "considering I don't have one."

"Oh dear," he replied. Then he added, "Perhaps it's not an uncle of yours, but of mine."

"Okay. Do *you* have an Uncle Woody?"

"No."

I gave him back the Communicator. "So what do we do now?"

The Professor was absorbed in his thoughts. His eyes narrowed, and he spoke barely above a whisper. "I remember something, long repressed… I was very little… virtually a toddler…there was a stuffed animal… a red bird with a demonic laugh… I was frightened and tried to get away but they kept putting him in my face! He laughed at me! The more I cried the more he laughed in my face! I will never forget that awful, mocking sound:

"'Heh-heh-heh HEH hooooo!
"'Heh-heh-heh *HEH* hooooo!!'

"And then, like a Gatlin gun:

"'Heh-heh-heh-heh-heh-heh-heh-heh!'

"I screamed in fear and rage, but he just kept laughing in my face:

"'Heh-heh-heh HEH hooooo!
"'Heh-heh-heh *HEH* hooooo!!
"'Heh-heh-heh-heh-heh-heh-heh-heh!'"

The Professor pulled out a handkerchief and mopped his brow. "I still break out in a cold sweat when I think about that Woody Pecker."

Then I remembered. I hadn't given him another thought since the day I fired him, a dozen years before. But now I could see him standing there, cameras rolling, as he told his audience, "Do it for your good ol' Uncle Woody!" I turned to my staff and we threw up our hands. People throughout West Michigan loved this guy, but my staff and I hated him and wanted him off the air. He was my science reporter, but he was the corniest guy I had ever known. On this occasion, he was giving his usual boosterish speech, urging his viewers to attend a science fair at a local high school. "Come on out and see what these young people have accomplished. Do it for your good ol' Uncle Woody, okay?"

One day he went too far. He wore a t-shirt on-air with the logo of a local company that had repeatedly refused to sponsor our program. He was giving them free air-time—an endorsement—and I fired him. My staff and I broke out the champagne afterwards. I received some angry mail from viewers, but it was worth it. Woody Wilson was out of my life for good. I never looked back.

"Not him," I muttered. "Anybody but him!"

The Professor emerged from his reverie. "Hm? What did you say?"

I considered my alternatives a moment. "These aliens will destroy the world, you say?"

He nodded. "And all its inhabitants."

I mulled it over. I hated that guy.

"Are you sure I'm supposed to contact this person?"

"Do you know who it is, Mr. Blayzak?"

"I think I do."

"All I can tell you is this. Whoever 'Uncle Woody' is, we need him. He's the next piece of this puzzle. He'll take us one step closer to finding

Basil and preventing disaster."

"Well," I said with a laugh, "I'll look him up. But don't get your hopes up about that last part. He's pretty good at bringing disaster upon himself."

10 THIS I WAS NOT EXPECTING

We took my shuttle back toward earth and stopped at a black market station to exchange it for another one. I didn't want anyone to track my whereabouts.

The new shuttle was an MV-500 series family van, capable of driving on roads as well as flying. It reminded me of an old RV camper with wings and rocket power. It wasn't stylish but it was roomy, and that's what I needed. I didn't want the Professor breathing down my neck the whole time.

During our descent through the earth's atmosphere, the Professor went to the back of the shuttle to use the facilities.

As soon as I was alone, I pulled out my phone and Skyped Naif. He answered immediately.

He was back on earth already. He had bummed a ride with The Cavalry.

"Where are you?" he asked.

"I can't tell you right now," I said. "I'm checking out a story with the Professor. Remember him? Long, dirty fingernails? Lives on the far side of the moon?"

"Oh, that guy. What kind of story?"

"Not sure yet. I'll let you know when I figure it out."

"Well, Dodge is having a fit about you. He doesn't like being the last to know something. Can't you tell me where you are?"

"Sorry, but the Professor says No. I'm allowing him to think I'm his hostage right now. Could turn into something interesting if we play along."

"Whatever you say, Dak. But you *have* heard the rumors, right? You know what people are saying about you—"

I was mad. "Not that hair plug thing again! What's it going to take to convince people—"

"No no no," said Naif. "Not that. This is much bigger. Everybody's looking for you. All the major networks and the smaller ones, too. For some reason, people think you're de—"

The Professor was coming. "Gotta go," I said, turning off my phone and hiding it in my pocket.

The Professor was upset when he rejoined me. "Curse those engineers! I almost flushed myself into space!"

Something had been on my mind, and I wanted to ask him about it. "Professor, what do they have against us? Why do they want to destroy us?"

He gave me a strange look. "I don't think that's their intention. But I wish they'd be more thoughtful of the end user."

I was confused. "Who are you talking about?"

"Who are *you* talking about?"

"Your alien friends. Why do they want to destroy the world? Do they not like us, or is this some awful, twisted game they're playing? 'Find Waldo or Die!'"

"His name is Basil, not Waldo."

I rolled my eyes. "I should've known you wouldn't get the joke. I just thought you'd appreciate the historical reference."

He sniffed. "I can't understand why you would want to make light of something like this. It's no laughing matter."

"I'll tell you the truth, Professor, and this time I'm not joking. I feel like we're committing treason. You should turn that Communicator over to the US government."

He was shocked. "Why?"

"Because a foreign power is threatening our world. They should've known enough to contact the proper authorities, but since they didn't, it's up to you and me to follow protocol."

"And why do you assume that the US government constitutes the 'proper authorities'?"

I shrugged. "Fine. Then take it to the United Nations. Some government agency. Haven't you ever seen the old movies about foreign invaders? They always say, 'Take me to your leader.'"

"I'm an expatriate," the Professor said. "I don't have a leader."

I shook my head. "You really have turned your back on the human race."

"I'm not ashamed to admit that," he said. "I no longer have any sympathy for this planet or its inhabitants. And I don't recognize its political leaders as authoritative. Neither do the aliens. They're dealing

35

directly with me... and now with you. We either cooperate with them or we'll be responsible for the consequences. As much as I hate humanity, I don't want the lives of trillions of people on my conscience."

"Nobly spoken," I said. "I'm sure you'll earn the undying thanks of the whole human race."

"I don't want it," he replied.

"Once again, I was joking. I've gotta remember not to do that with you."

West Michigan's population exploded in the first half of the twenty-first century, during the Second Civil War. Eager to escape the hostilities, a few million people left big cities all across the country to move to Holland, Michigan, a place where old-fashioned community values were still on display. There, on Lake Michigan's eastern shore, architects erected a futuristic skyline that made both Milwaukee's and Chicago's seem behind the times. Of course, that was exactly what all those people were trying to get away from, so now they moved inland. In less than ten years, the entire western half of Michigan became one big mass of contiguous suburbs where people tried against all odds to revive the small-town way of life.

My first big break in the news industry took place in the West Michigan Megaland, about twenty years after the population explosion. I took over as anchor and bureau chief of the local GNN affiliate, WKNR. I was young and cocky, and I was determined to be noticed. I wanted to be where the action was, and if West Michigan prided itself on its small-town values, then it was my job to shake things up.

Woody Wilson had been around for a long time when I took over. He was the science reporter, but I called him our pseudo-science guy. He looked just like Albert Einstein—an image he cultivated intentionally—and he was extremely personable. People loved him, but I wanted him out. I was striving for an edgier news program, and I wanted our segments to go viral on a regular basis. It wasn't all investigative journalism, although that was my stock-in-trade. We did think pieces, too. But everything we did had to be relevant to a global audience, and Woody Wilson did not have international potential.

When I fired him, I was surprised by the number of viewers who protested. Thousands. I really didn't think there were that many hicks left in the Megaland. Of course, I didn't let them sway me, because I never considered Michiganians (or Michiganders, as some of them called themselves) my true audience base. I was from Cleveland, and I relied on viewers from all over the country and the world, and they didn't let me down. By following that strategy, I became GNN's number one investigative reporter. I didn't let guys like Woody Wilson stand in my way.

So now here I was, sitting voluntarily in a shuttle, moving at high speed toward a reunion with the man I had fired.

I tried to imagine how he would react. Would he turn us away with a snarl and tell us never to darken his door again? That's what *I* would've done if he had shown up at *my* door, but that didn't seem like his style. I considered it more likely that he'd invite us in but he'd be curt. I could accept that. My preference, however, would be for him to act like nothing had ever happened between us. I'd explain our errand in a businesslike manner and he'd comply with our wishes. The more I thought about it, the more I hoped that it worked out just like that.

The shuttle was slowing down now, descending to street level. We were in an old-fashioned neighborhood. All the houses were at least a hundred years old. Mid-twentieth century. Very behind-the-times. The Professor should have felt quite at home.

We stopped in front of a dumpy little ranch-style house on a quiet street. There were strange gadgets in the yard and on the roof: cameras, telescopes, solar panels, satellite dishes—all jerry-rigged.

We climbed out of the shuttle and hurried to the front door.

"Let's do this as quietly as we can," the Professor told me.

I rang the doorbell, and Woody answered. He had hardly changed at all. He still looked like Einstein. There was no sign of recognition on his face, but he greeted us with a warm smile.

"Hello, Woody," I said. "Do you remember me?"

Suddenly he did, and he was elated. Throwing his arms around me, he gave me the tightest bear hug I've ever had, lifting me off my feet.

"You're alive!" he said, jumping up and down with me. "You're alive!"

This I was not expecting.

11 THE TINKERER AND HIS TOYS

Out of the corner of my eye, I could see the Professor staring in disbelief.

"Edna!" Woody cried. "Look who's here!"

Woody's wife hurried to the door. She was a roundish woman, the kind who must've always looked like somebody's aunt, even when she was thirteen.

"Mercy!" she said in a shrill voice. "Dak Blayzak! You *are* alive!"

The Professor glanced nervously at the surrounding houses and whispered that we should get inside before others took notice.

Soon we were in their living room. I introduced the Professor, but Woody wasn't paying attention.

"Dak! I've become an inventor since I retired!"

So he *retired*, did he?

"Let me show you what I've been working on!" he said, and he led the Professor and me downstairs to his basement. There were machines everywhere, some only partly completed, with wires sticking out of them.

He picked up a saxophone that had an electrical cord coming out of it. The other end of the cord was attached to an old-fashioned wall socket.

"There's no other tenor sax in the world like this one," he said. "I rigged it up myself. If you make a mistake, it corrects you with a little zap. Just a small one. Nothing serious. If you make it a second time, it zaps you a little harder, and so on. It's harmless, but it teaches you not to make that mistake again, let me tell you!"

He brought the instrument to his lips and began to play. He was doing fine until he missed a sharp. "Ouch!" he said. "I'll try again."

He replayed the passage and missed the same note. "OWWW!"

He laughed. "It really does drive the point home. This time I'll get it right."

He didn't, but after he missed the note he did stop playing. With the instrument still in his mouth, he stared straight ahead. His eyes became bigger and bigger.

"Woody?"

After a moment of silence, I walked up to him and stared in his face. A wisp of smoke was rising from his hair.

"Woody!"

The Professor yanked the extension cord out of the wall, and Woody shook his head vigorously. "Guess I'll have to turn it down a little."

"We're wasting time!" the Professor told me.

Woody walked over to a dart board on the wall and detached one of the darts. "Here's another one of my inventions," he said. "It's a Smart Dart. If someone invites you to play, you can join in worry-free, even if you couldn't hit the side of a barn. It's programmed for circle recognition."

"Will it hit the bull's-eye?" I asked.

"Not necessarily. Since the target has circles inside of circles, the dart has to make a choice. I haven't told it whether to prefer the outer or inner ones. I honestly don't know whether it will choose big or small circles. Let's see what it does."

Just as he threw it, the Professor bent over to grab his burlap sack. The dart veered sharply to the right and attached itself to the Professor's hind quarters. He bellowed pathetically.

"Looks like it prefers big ones," I said.

The Professor was not amused. "The future of the planet is at stake, and we're playing children's games!"

Woody turned to me. "What's he talking about? And what's he got in that bag?"

"The hope of the world!" the Professor said.

Woody gave me a look that spoke volumes.

"Better humor him," I said. "He's armed."

The Professor held out the Communicator.

"What on *earth* is that?" Woody asked.

"It's not *from* earth," the Professor told him. "It's from another world."

Woody looked at me again, this time with dismay.

"It's a communication device," the Professor continued. "It has warned me about an impending catastrophe. We have a chance to prevent it, but we need your cooperation."

Woody balked. "Who's 'we'? And what do you want from me?"

The Professor sighed. "I was quite content to save the world myself, but this device told me I needed the assistance of Mr. Blayzak. When *he* inquired of it, it told him to contact you. Now we need you to consult it."

Woody turned his back on the Professor and paced the length of the basement. On his return, he stopped and glared at me, then turned to the Professor. "I don't play with Ouija boards."

The Professor was so angry, he couldn't speak.

"Woody," I said, "I didn't believe it either. I'm still not sure what I think about it. But this man is a professor—I can vouch for that—and he and I are looking for somebody. I know it sounds strange, but we have reason to believe that you can help us find him."

"What's his name?"

I glanced at the Professor but decided I'd better field this one myself. "All we know is that his name is Basil."

Woody waited, but that was all the information I had. So he paced again, then came back to me. "I'm sorry. I can't help you. I don't know anyone named Basil."

The Professor's patience was running out. "That's not the point. We don't know him, either. But the Communicator will help us find him if you cooperate."

Woody bristled. "What do you want me to do?"

I tried to speak soothingly. "We just want you to hold onto the device with both hands. A message will appear on the panel, and the Professor will read it. There's nothing to it."

Woody shook his head. "Neither of you are making any sense."

"Probably not," I said, "but I've never known you to refuse something new. Why don't you just give it a try? It won't zap you."

"I'm sure it won't," he said. "That's not what worries me."

"What's the problem, then?" the Professor demanded.

Woody looked him right in the eyes. "The problem is that you're a quack, and I don't cooperate with quacks." He turned to me and added, "And you should know me better than that." Then he marched to the corner of the room and stood with his back to us.

12 IMPOSTOR

The Professor looked at me and I shrugged. Then I got an idea.

"Woody," I said, "I'm asking for your help figuring this guy out."

He still had his back to me, but his head cocked slightly, so I continued.

"Somehow, when I held onto that Communicator, it told the Professor about you. He had never heard of you before, but the Communicator mentioned you by name. I don't know how that's possible. Maybe you can figure it out."

"Oldest trick in the book, Dak. Psychics do that kind of thing all the time. They get you talking until you volunteer the information they're looking for."

"I don't know, Woody. I can't figure out how he did it. If he really is a quack and this whole thing is a hoax, I need your help to come to the bottom of it. If he's wrong, let's prove him wrong together."

Woody turned in my direction slightly. "You had me worried, Dak. First I hear you're dead, then you turn up with this Svengali person—"

The Professor exploded. "How dare you!"

"But if I can help you, Dak, I'll do it. I'll show you that he's an imposter. And if I do, do you promise me you'll walk away from him and stop listening to his lies?"

"I promise, Woody."

That was all it took. "Okay," he said. "Hand it over, Doc."

"It doesn't work that way," the Professor said with a snarl. "I have to read the message that appears on the monitor."

"See, Dak? He won't relinquish control. That's your first clue. If we don't do it his way, it won't work. Pretty obvious, don't you think?"

"Fine," said the Professor, handing him the Communicator. "Take it.

But you won't be able to read it."

"Of course not," said Woody. "Neither can you. But you put on a good show."

Woody took the Communicator and brought it over to me. "Now watch," he said.

He grasped each end of the device and we looked at the monitor together. Some strange pictograms appeared on the screen.

Woody was mildly surprised. "Is this the same message it showed you?" he asked me.

"No," I said. "Mine was different."

"Interesting..." He turned to the Professor. "How'd you make this thing, Doc?"

"I didn't, you little—" The Professor stopped himself. "You're holding a mystery you'll never understand."

"Hmmm. So, Dak, I suppose the Professor here is the only one in the world who can decipher this code, is that right?"

The Professor's hands tightened into fists. "It's an ancient Mesopotamian language that was lost to history until I reconstructed it. No one else has mastered it yet."

"Of course," Woody said with a smile. "Of course."

I decided to help the Professor out before he became violent. "Woody, I did a segment on this guy months ago. Several noted philologists told me that his work is genuine. He's eccentric, but his credentials are impeccable."

Woody spoke sympathetically. "Now, now, Dak. Be strong."

"We're wasting time!" the Professor said, stomping over to us. "What does the Communicator say?"

"*You* tell *me*, Doc."

The Professor looked hard at the monitor a moment. "The first character refers to an exceptionally intelligent boy."

"Hmpf!" Woody said, grinning at me. "See how this works? You've probably told him about my volunteer work with young people."

"We didn't discuss that, Woody, but I do remember that you used to be a mentor."

"Yes, I was a local celebrity, and bright kids came to me in droves. I always encouraged them to think scientifically in every aspect of their lives. I considered it my civic duty, passing the love of science on to the next generation. Anybody who's heard of me knows about that, Dak. Your Professor here has done his homework, I'll give him credit for that."

The Professor looked again at the monitor and muttered. "Oh no."

"What's the matter, Doc?" said Woody.

The Professor glanced at me and grimaced. "Now it's trying to convey the name phonetically. It says, 'Lem... lem... lemma... '" He stared at me helplessly. "You can't possibly understand how difficult this is."

Woody laughed. "Notice what he's doing, Dak? He wants us to finish the word for him. Let's just see what he comes up with on his own."

"'Lemma-*uhnn*."

Pause.

"Lemma-un-*juuuh*...'"

He took a deep breath and started over: "'Lemma-un-juh-*ullll*...'"

Another long pause.

"Lemma-un-juh-ulll-*oh*...'"

He tried again:

"'Lem... un... jullll... oh...' 'Lem... un... jullll... oh...'"

At last the Professor looked solemnly into Woody's eyes and announced, "The boy's name is Lemon Jello."

Woody handed the Communicator back to the Professor and paced the room several times. Then he rejoined us. "I know a Velvet Brown. I've met a Chandra Lear. I've even spoken with a Jack Daniels. But I do not know anyone named Lemon Jello."

I turned to the Professor. "Could there be a mistake?"

He waived at the Communicator. "Would *you* like to try?"

Woody walked to the foot of the stairs and called to his wife. "Do I know a boy genius by the name of Lemon Jello?"

There was no reply, and Woody grinned at us triumphantly. Then his wife shouted back, "Do you mean L'Monjello?"

Woody stiffened thoughtfully. "L'Monjello! Black kid... Really short for his age... Smartest little guy I ever met... Everything he did was brilliant... I promised to help him on a project, but I couldn't. He kept badgering me about it, but I didn't even know where to start. I never had the nerve to tell him... What was he trying to do? I don't remember... I never got back to him... Poor kid. Must've broke his little heart..."

"Woody."

He tore himself free from his reverie and looked at me.

"Where is L'Monjello now?"

He shook his head. "I don't know. I lost track of him years ago."

"Do you remember his last name?"

"Parker," his wife shouted from upstairs.

Woody and I faced each other a moment, and I didn't have to say a word.

"Okay, Dak. I'll look him up. But you better keep the Professor in the background or that kid will never cooperate. He's too smart to fall for this."

"Is that what you're doing? Falling for it?"

Woody was thoughtful for a moment. "I don't know how Svengali wrangled it out of me, but that doesn't matter. I promised little L'Monjello I'd help him, and I didn't keep my promise. I've been meaning to do something about it for years. It's time I stopped saying that. Help me find him, Dak, and I'll make it up to him somehow."

He stared off into space. "Little L'Monjello... Poor kid!"

13 THE STAR STUDENT

When it first opened its doors in the last half of the twentieth century, Valley University was a small campus in the country, far from any metropolitan area. Now it was a sprawling campus, surrounded by Megaland communities. Like many twenty-first century universities, it was now built entirely around student life. The old lecture halls of a previous era were gone. Multimedia teaching aids were now available online, presented by world-class celebrity scholars, most of whom were so busy with research, the students never met them. The campus was a place for students to gather and support each other in mostly self-guided instruction. Professors supervised student projects, but students rarely formed relationships with them. They looked to each other for help—especially to the so-called "star students."

At The Valley, senior L'Monjello Parker was one of those stars. Everybody knew him, and that made it easy for us to find him.

As our shuttle descended over The Valley, the Professor seemed agitated. He clearly did not like being in a university setting again.

We landed in a field just off-campus, hoping not to attract too much attention to our shuttle. As we stepped out, the Professor worried that I'd be recognized.

"I've got just the thing," I said, and I pulled out the fake moustache and glasses I used for just such moments.

Woody took one look and tried not to laugh.

"What?" I said.

We must've been quite a sight as we marched across campus: the Professor with his burlap sack, me with my fake moustache and glasses, and Albert Einstein.

When we found the apartment, the Professor and I stood back and let

Woody ring the doorbell.

A young black man opened the door. He was huge: over six feet tall and all muscle. He nearly filled the doorway, and when he spoke, his voice boomed.

"You boys lost?" he asked.

Woody answered. "We're looking for L'Monjello Parker."

"You've found him," the giant replied.

Woody stood there in disbelief. "But...but... you're so..." His mouth formed the letter B, but he was so shocked, he couldn't come out with it.

So L'Monjello helped him out. "Black? Yes I am. And you're not, little white man. I'm so sorry."

Woody laughed slightly. "No, I mean... you're just so—"

"Beautiful? Aw, stop. You're making me blush."

Woody turned back to the Professor and me for help, but we urged him to keep trying.

He shook his head and said, "I'm just surprised, that's all. You're so..."

"Brilliant? Guilty as charged. Now... let's get down to business. What are you boys selling?"

Woody held up both hands and said, "L'Monjello. It's me... Woody Wilson."

The young man's face became serious and he stooped down to look into the older man's eyes. *"Woody? But... you're so... little!"*

L'Monjello ran around the room grabbing books and papers so we could all sit down. "Sorry about messin' with you like that," he said. "I love salesmen."

Once we were seated, he said, "So..." Then he nodded and waited for Woody to finish the sentence.

"So..." Woody said, nodding back.

We all sat there.

Finally L'Monjello said, "You boys thirsty? Hungry?"

We shook our heads.

"Good, good... Fridge is empty anyway... So... Woody... um..." He sat there a moment, waiting, then said, "Wassup?"

"Not much, L'Monjello. Not much."

"Oh..." They both nodded again. "Okay..."

I nudged Woody and pointed at the burlap sack. He shook his head and whispered, "Not yet."

He cleared his throat. "L'Monjello... I've been trying to remember

46

something. You were working on a project. You asked me to help you with it. I can't quite remember what it was."

The young man stared at him a moment. "Are you talking about that Lilienthal Glider I was building?"

Woody slapped his knee. "That's what it was!"

L'Monjello nodded, shook his head, and nodded again. "Um... okay."

Woody turned to the Professor and me. "Otto Lilienthal had a flying machine in the works before the Wright Brothers made history with theirs. L'Monjello was building his own Lilienthal Glider. He wanted to see what was wrong with it." He turned back to L'Monjello and added, "Quite impressive, really."

The young man nodded again. "Um... okay... thanks... um..."

Now the Professor cleared his throat, and L'Monjello turned to look him over. Then his eyes rested on me. I was still wearing my fake moustache and glasses. "Where'd you pick up Groucho Marx?"

"Hm?" Woody said. Then he glanced at me and laughed. "Oh! No... that's Dak Blayzak."

L'Monjello was skeptical. "He's dead, isn't he?"

I turned to the Professor. "Have I missed something?"

But the Professor had been silent long enough. "Mister Wilson, if you would please get down to business."

L'Monjello laughed and mimicked the Professor. "Yes, Mister Wilson, if you please... Tell me what's going on."

Woody had a hard time saying what was on his mind. "Well you see, L'Monjello, it's like this. I know you wanted me to help you, and I've never forgotten that, and... well... I know it's been a while but... here I am."

They looked at each other for a moment, and finally L'Monjello said, "Wow."

Another moment passed. Then he said it again.

"Wow."

"I came as soon as I could."

"Really? 'Cause it's been eleven years. You must have one helluva To-Do List."

Woody didn't know what to say. Finally, in a deep, broken voice, he whispered, "Sorry."

L'Monjello nodded. "Hey... yeah... it's okay, Woody. I mean, it hurt at the time, but I'm over it. I'm not mad at you."

Woody nodded gratefully. He seemed genuinely relieved.

L'Monjello looked around at the rest of us. "Is that it? Are we done here?"

The Professor reached over and dropped the burlap sack in Woody's lap.

"Actually," I said, "there's something else."

L'Monjello eyed the bag suspiciously. "You got a bomb in there?"

Woody laughed. "No," he said. "I'm not exactly sure what it is. I was hoping you'd help me figure it out." And taking the Communicator out of the bag, he handed it to his young friend.

L'Monjello was greatly intrigued. He turned it over and over in his hands, looking at it from every angle. "What kind of metal is this?" he asked.

Woody shook his head. "What do *you* think?"

"No clue," said L'Monjello. "Was it created on a space station?"

We were all surprised. "Why do you ask?"

"It reminds me of a material I handled a few years ago, something they made outside the earth's atmosphere. It was unfamiliar to the touch. Just like this is."

He turned it this way and that to see how the light hit it. "What's it used for?"

Woody pointed. "Put your hands on either end of it, and see what happens."

L'Monjello did as he was told, and pictograms appeared on the monitor. "Ah-ha! Is it some sort of e-Reader? Can we change it to English?"

Woody gestured toward the Professor. "This gentleman is an expert in ancient Sumerian languages. He found this device buried beneath the ground, on the far side of the moon."

L'Monjello turned to the Professor. "Can you read this language?"

The Professor nodded.

"Well enough to decipher what this thing is?"

"Yes."

L'Monjello turned back to Woody, surprised. "So why are you asking me?"

The Professor spoke up. "Because he doesn't believe what I told him."

"Which is?"

"That it's a communication device. And that I use it to speak with aliens from another world."

Woody and I rolled our eyes, and L'Monjello suppressed a grin. "I see." He regarded the device with renewed interest. "And what other world is that, may I ask?"

The Professor didn't know how to respond, so L'Monjello tried a different question.

"What galaxy have you been communicating with?"

The Professor stammered. "I... I'm... not sure..."

L'Monjello glanced at Woody and winked. "How can you be sure you're talking to aliens from another galaxy if you don't know where they're calling from?"

The Professor's face turned red. "They don't say they're from another galaxy. They talk as if they're gods. But I don't believe them."

"Good for you!" L'Monjello replied. "A little skepticism is healthy when you're conversing with aliens from another world."

Woody and I laughed. The Professor was trying so hard to keep silent, a strange gurgling sound came out of his throat.

L'Monjello reached for his pocket knife and started to scratch the surface of the Communicator. "Let me get some shavings of this and put it under my microscope."

The Professor jumped up and grabbed the device from his hands. "How dare you! You hold the future of this planet in your hands!"

"What's the problem?" I asked sternly.

"They warned me," he replied, clutching the device tightly to his breast. "If any harm should come to this Communicator..."

"Then what?"

He looked terrified. "Immediate response! Flames will encircle the globe... and all flesh shall see it."

"Why didn't you tell me this before?"

"You didn't need to know."

"Didn't I?" I thought a moment. "What else haven't you told me?"

He didn't answer, and I couldn't hold my tongue. "Are you making all this up as you go along?"

He looked deeply wounded, but his voice was husky. "I don't care what you think of me—what any of you think—but I must protect this device with my life."

Stuffing the Communicator back into the burlap sack, he stormed out of the apartment and ran down the street.

14 TO TRUST OR NOT TO TRUST

The gravity of my situation hit me with full force. I was the Internet's Number One investigative journalist, and I was sacrificing my reputation on the testimony of this one man. What if Woody was right? What if he was a crackpot? When word got out about this, I'd be ruined.

"Where's he going?" Woody asked, watching out the window.

I sighed. "He probably needs time to clear his mind. He'll be back."

Woody turned to L'Monjello. "What do you think that contraption is? How do you think it works?"

"I don't know. And I guess I'm not going to find out if I can't get my hands on it again."

"But let's think about this," said Woody. "The Professor digs it up on the far side of the moon. How did it get there?"

"Do we know for a fact that that's where he got it?"

I butted in. "I didn't see him dig it up, but he was on the far side of the moon when I found him."

Woody added, "And you said yourself that it had an extra-terrestrial quality to it."

"Yes I did," L'Monjello admitted.

Woody continued. "Now here we have this Professor who thinks he's got this unique relationship with alien creatures, and then he gets a memo from them. They tell him to go find Dak. Think about that a moment. He believed he was going to save the world all by himself, and then he gets this very disappointing message. It's disappointing not only because he wants to work alone, but also because he doesn't like Dak. Am I right, Dak?"

"Probably," I said. "The reverse is certainly true."

"So if the Professor was making all this up, would he have gone looking for Dak? I don't think so. Here's something else: he's no sooner told to go find Dak than—*presto!*—Dak shows up."

L'Monjello turned to me. "Really? What were you doing there?"

I couldn't tell them about Deep Throat, of course. "It's a long story," I said.

"Now it gets even more interesting," Woody continued, "because Dak talks to the Communicator and it tells him to go find *me!* And I was probably the last person on earth he wanted to go looking for. Am I right, Dak?"

There was no point in trying to be polite. "The second-to-the-last," I said, remembering the Professor.

"Really?" said L'Monjello. "Why didn't Dak want to talk to you?"

"Because he fired me years ago. It was all the buzz at the time."

"Oh yeah. I remember that. Shame on you, Dak!"

Woody turned to me. "Be honest. Would you have sought me out if the Communicator hadn't told you to do it?"

I shook my head.

"So Dak and the Professor come to see me, and who does the Communicator tell me to look up? You!"

L'Monjello grinned. "And I was the last person on earth you wanted to talk to, is that what you're telling me?"

"Well..."

"I understand. You blew me off years ago, and now the Communicator told you to come and make amends, is that it?"

I didn't like where this was headed. "You two are missing the point. It's not about making amends. It's about finding this alien—if there is an alien—and preventing the world from being destroyed. As I understand it, we're all just links in the chain. Somewhere down the line, someone will know the alien."

"But how many links will it take?" Woody asked. "We could be doing this for years."

"If the Professor's telling the truth, then we have no more than ten days. Make that seven. It was ten when the Professor started out. If we don't find Basil by the 24th, we're dead."

L'Monjello was thoughtful a moment. "Even so, Dak, there's a definite pattern here. Every link in the chain so far has been someone that the previous person wanted to avoid. The Professor wanted to avoid you, you wanted to avoid Woody, Woody wanted to avoid me..."

"So are you worried about what the Communicator will tell you?" Woody asked.

"You bet I am!" he said. "But I'm also not convinced that the Professor's story is true... or that he's entirely sane."

"Neither am I," Woody said.

"I'm still on the fence," I admitted. "But if he's telling the truth, he needs all the help he can get."

"Right," said L'Monjello, "and that's the only reason I'm going along with it. But consider this. What if he's crazy... and the images on this Communicator are like a Rorschach test? What if it's a kind of ink blot, and we read our own concerns into it? You felt guilty about me, Woody, so that's what appeared on the screen. And you felt guilty about Woody, Dak, so his name came up. And so on. Makes sense, doesn't it?"

Woody thought so, but I didn't. "There are too many problems with that theory. First, we aren't the ones reading the ink blot. The Professor's doing that."

"Yes," said Woody, "but I told you all along, he's manipulating us somehow. We're feeding him information, and he's building on it. That's my suspicion."

"I don't think so," I said. "You were careful not to give him any clues, Woody. He came up with Lemon Jello all on his own."

"Huh?" said L'Monjello.

"Second, I didn't feel the least bit guilty about firing you, Woody. Sorry, but it's true. And when the Professor read your name on the Communicator, I didn't even remember you at first."

Woody snorted. "Thanks a lot!"

"And if *you're* being honest, you weren't sitting around moping about L'Monjello, either. Your wife remembered him before you did."

"Well that's because I've never heard him called Lemon Jello."

L'Monjello shook his head. "What are you two talking about?"

"Third, I went to the far side of the moon because I had it on good advice that a story of major importance was about to break. The person who gave me that tip has never been wrong."

Woody was weakening.

"Finally, the Professor may be eccentric and self-absorbed, but he's not out to fool people. He'd rather spend the rest of his life in isolation, far from human contact, than lead a bunch of pilgrims on a fieldtrip to Nowhere. He's only doing it for one reason: because he believes what he's telling us."

L'Monjello nodded. "And if you're right, then we only have to worry about one thing: that he himself may be mistaken."

"Deranged, you mean," said Woody.

"Whatever you want to call it," said L'Monjello. "But I agree with Dak. I don't think he's intentionally deceiving us. If he's not telling the truth, it's because he's deceiving himself."

The door opened, and the Professor came back in.

We all sat in silence as he stood there a moment. Finally he spoke. "I wanted to walk away and never come back. But I need your help. I wish I didn't, but I do."

He turned to L'Monjello.

"Mr. Parker, I know you're curious about this device. If circumstances were different, I would be quite willing to let you examine it in greater detail. Perhaps you could answer some questions I've wondered about myself. But I have a job to do, and I'm going to do it if it costs me my life."

We all glanced at each other.

"Will you help me, young man?"

L'Monjello studied the Professor's face quite seriously, then he nodded. "Yes, sir. I'll help you."

15 CHEESY

When L'Monjello took the Communicator in his hands, he tried to put on his poker face.

The Professor studied the monitor a moment and seemed quite interested in what it showed him. "There are two characters here," he said, pointing at them. "If I'm interpreting them correctly, they are opposing descriptions of a single person."

L'Monjello remained silent and expressionless.

"They also both refer to cheese," the Professor added.

At that point, none of us could keep a straight face, not even L'Monjello.

Woody said, "Lemon Jello, Cheese... What's next—Crackers?"

"I fail to see the humor in this," the Professor said.

L'Monjello tried to be conciliatory, but he couldn't stop laughing. "I'm sorry, Professor. Don't mind them. This is very interesting. And I... I mean that. Truly. Now... exactly what is the Communicator trying to tell you?"

Woody blurted out, "That the moon's made of Green Cheese!"

Now we were just getting silly, but we couldn't stop laughing.

L'Monjello struggled to control himself. "Just ignore them, Professor. You say the two characters are in opposition to each other?"

The Professor was not happy, but he answered the question. "Yes, apparently. This first one refers to a cheap, tawdry kind of character—probably female. If I'm not mistaken, it would be equivalent to our word 'cheesecake.' But the second connotes elegance... a delicacy... 'Brie' would be my guess."

L'Monjello was suddenly serious. He looked like he was thinking through the steps of a complex math problem. Handing the

Communicator back to the Professor, he rubbed his chin a moment, then he approached Woody and me. "Did you two see... Did I... Could you tell if I gave him any clues?"

We shook our heads.

He stared off into space a moment, then returned to the Professor and extended his hand. "I was wrong about you," he said. "Please accept my apology."

The Professor didn't know whether the young man was mocking him, but after a moment's hesitation he shook L'Monjello's hand.

Grabbing a remote, L'Monjello turned on the TV. "This is the one channel I watch faithfully, day and night. Sometimes I flick the dial now and then, but I always come back to her."

It was a Home Channel—an amateur Reality-TV network. A pale-skinned girl with long blonde hair was shown lounging in provocative clothing, and a female announcer said in a breathy voice, "You're watching... Brie." Her name was featured in shining gold letters.

Woody wasn't joking anymore. "She's beautiful," he said.

"A veritable goddess," said the Professor.

"Who is she?" I asked.

L'Monjello sighed. "She's a student here. I loved her the moment I saw her. I'm not ashamed to say that. I caught a glimpse of her at the library my junior year. Of course, she was surrounded by her camera crew, but I saw her through the crowd and..." He threw up his hands. "That was it."

Woody and I glanced at the Professor, at each other, then back at L'Monjello. Nobody dared to say it.

The young man sank back into the couch and put his head in his hands. "Look, guys, I know what you're thinking. You want me to take the Communicator to her."

We were silent.

"Well, let me tell you something. I've tried to meet her, and it can't be done. Her people have a screening process. They won't let me get anywhere near her. I've tried."

He told us about all the different ways he had tried to meet her, and how each attempt had ended in failure.

"Months passed," he said. "Then I got an idea. I applied! There's an application on her website. If you want to meet her, you've got to be on the show, of course, because she's on camera most of the time. So I filled out an application and somebody came to interview me. They had a camera rolling the whole time. A few weeks later they sent me a form letter and said I lacked on-screen charisma. And that was the end of it."

He walked over to the TV. "She's my angel, but I'll never meet her."

And with a press of the remote, the screen went black.

The Professor dragged me over to a corner of the room and said, "We've got to get them together. The survival of the world is at stake!"

"Okay, Cupid. Got any arrows in that burlap sack?"

"I'm not joking."

"You never are."

"I can hear everything you're saying," L'Monjello told us.

Woody spoke up. "Why not have Dak interview her? She'd probably jump at that. Sorry, L'Monjello, but the point is to get the Communicator into her hands, isn't it?"

"No it's not," said the Professor. "Only Mr. Parker can do this."

"How do you know that?" I asked. "You keep coming up with these rules that you didn't mention before."

"I just know," he said. "When the Communicator tells you the name of a person, it is you who must contact them. You're the one who knows them. You're the one who has to do it. No one else can do it for you."

There was silence a moment, then all eyes turned to L'Monjello.

He shook his head. "I never should've let you boys in."

16 THE KIDNAPPERS' PLOT

We sat around the TV, watching her as she went about her errands. I was bored already.

"What does she do all day?" I asked.

"Whatever her writers come up with," L'Monjello said. "It's all scripted."

Today she and her friends were solving some sort of Nancy Drew-type mystery. Some of the others were pretty good actors, but she wasn't. She kept turning to the Teleprompter.

When Woody and I were alone for a moment, I asked him, "What does he see in her? L'Monjello's a smart guy. Doesn't he realize she's no good for him?"

"How do you know that?"

"She's no intellectual heavyweight, Woody, in case you didn't notice."

"You are so judgmental!" he said.

"Well, it's true. And her show is so corny. Who writes that stuff?"

"Not her—obviously. But she's graceful and poised and her voice sounds like music. I can certainly understand why L'Monjello's in love with her."

We joined the others again and glanced at the TV.

"Is this live?" Woody asked.

"Yes."

I looked out the window. "Where's it taking place? Near here?"

He seemed worried. "It's not that simple, Dak. She's not part of the regular dorm system. You can't just walk down the street and knock on her door."

"Don't be so jittery," I told him. "I'm just asking."

Woody pointed at the screen. "But L'Monjello, look! She's at the fitness center."

"It's fake, Woody. It's actually part of her TV studio. She would never mingle with the rest of us. Believe me, if it was that simple, I'd have met her a long time ago. Our only chance to get anywhere near her will be at a public appearance."

"How often does that happen?" I asked.

"It's rare. But tomorrow's the Botball match with Ferris, and she's doing the halftime show."

"Really?" said Woody. "What does she do?"

"Song and dance. She's got some great moves, but I like her ballads. She has a beautiful voice."

I didn't get it. "And what do you think *we're* going to do? Go on stage and dance with her?"

"I don't know," he said. "I thought we might get to her before she goes out on the field."

"How?"

He shrugged. "All I know is this. On a normal day, we'd have to wade through multiple levels of crewmembers even to catch a glimpse of her. She's extremely cut off from the rest of the world. But when she goes out in public, it's just her bodyguards and her—"

"Bodyguards!" Woody said. "How are we supposed to get past *them*?"

L'Monjello sighed. "Look. I told you guys this was impossible. If you can think of a way to do it, I'll be glad to hear it. But don't expect me to have the answers."

We all looked around at each other. Nobody said anything for a while.

At last the Professor spoke. "On the 24th of this month, the world will end. The four of us have been given the opportunity to stop that from happening. We must let no obstacle prevent us from doing so. We need that girl."

He fixed his eyes upon L'Monjello and continued. "Whatever it takes, Mr. Parker, we must do it. If we must risk our reputations—or even our lives—so be it. But we must get the Communicator to that girl."

L'Monjello's gaze was just as stern. "First of all, Professor, I defy you to find a way to do it. But second, it sounds like you're talking about kidnapping her. That's a crime. And if we cross the state line with her, it's a federal offense. We'll all end up in prison."

Woody shrugged. "You want to meet her, don't you?"

"I want her to like me—not hate me!"

The Professor opened his mouth, but L'Monjello stopped him. "Don't tell me it's for the sake of the planet. She's everything to me, and I'm not going to let you take her against her will. Don't tell me it's for some greater good."

"This won't work without you," I told him.

"Then find another way."

We were all quiet for a moment, then I turned to the Professor. "I understand that L'Monjello has to be the one to talk to her, but are you sure we can't clear the path for him?"

The Professor was interested. "What do you have in mind?"

"Woody had a good idea. He thought I should offer to interview her. What if I worked it out with her people, just to get us in the door? L'Monjello could pose as a member of my crew. Once we're in, he could introduce himself and..."

"And what?" L'Monjello asked.

"Well," I said. "You could..."

Woody jumped in. "Tell her you'd like her autograph. Digitally. On this device you happen to have with you. It's right here in this burlap sack."

We lost it—all of us except the Professor.

He just scowled. "In answer to your question, Mr. Blayzak, I don't see any reason why you couldn't make arrangements with her producers. But after that it's got to be in Mr. Parker's hands. He'll have to find a way to get her to cooperate. I don't understand everything about this process, but there's something about the human contact that's essential. We mustn't interfere with that."

"What are you saying?" Woody asked. "Does he have to bond with her?"

The Professor thought a moment, then shook his head. "I don't know."

I stared at him. "You... don't... know."

"No. I don't."

"Dammit, Professor! You *have* to know. We're depending on you."

"I understand that, Mr. Blayzak. I'm drawing inferences from all of this, just as you are. But I'm sensing something... as if they're trying to tell me... and it's crucial that the links in this chain remain personal."

I glanced at L'Monjello and he held up his hands. Woody shrugged.

"Okay," I said. "If you're willing to let me get things started, then let's do it." I turned to L'Monjello. "How do I contact her people?"

"They've got an online form," he said, "but I don't recommend it. That'll take too long. Her PR person is a lady named Tamra Taransky, but her email address isn't public. Your best bet will be to walk up to her at the game tomorrow. I can point her out to you." He looked around at us and added, "But we need a backup plan, in case this doesn't work."

"Do you have another idea?" I asked.

He shook his head, but I could see that he did. He just didn't want to tell us what it was.

17 WHAT THE WAR WAS ABOUT

L'Monjello's apartment bustled with activity after that. When he wasn't on the phone making arrangements, friends were at his door bringing him supplies—food, a portable pillow, an unopened toothbrush—and from time to time he took them out to our shuttle.

"Hey," he said when we asked him about it. "I want her to feel at home."

"He certainly does plan ahead," I told the others.

"Yes," said Woody. "But I think he also wants to keep busy. He looks scared to death."

"I don't blame him," I said. "So am I."

Late in the evening, Woody handed his phone to me. "Look at this paper L'Monjello's been writing for his American History class. I asked him to send me a copy of it. I found it quite provocative."

I read the first paragraph and couldn't conceal my disgust. Turning to L'Monjello, I said, "If this is a joke, I'm not laughing. I take this subject very seriously."

"So do I," he said.

It was about the Second Civil War. And in his opening paragraph, he claimed that it had already started in the 1990s.

"Do you mean to tell me that people were living through a war and didn't even know it?"

He shook his head. "Don't think of it as a traditional war. It wasn't. It was a Civil Conflict. There was a lot of bloodshed, but it went far deeper than that. We came apart as a nation during those years, Dak. You ask me how that was possible—how people could be in the middle of something like that and not know it. I'm telling you... *they knew!* They just didn't know what to call it."

Woody shook his head. "Day after day, somebody entered a public place with an assault rifle and killed people. How could they not have known?"

L'Monjello turned to him. "It wasn't just with guns, Woody. They used their vehicles as weapons because they couldn't share the road. They built bombs and put them in backpacks."

"You're confusing separate issues," I said: "terrorism, road rage, people who just went berserk. Those were all different things."

L'Monjello was adamant. "That's what they told themselves at the time. They lacked the conceptual framework for understanding what was happening. Yes, the violence took on a wide variety of forms, but that wasn't the point. The social fabric was unraveling. Republicans and Democrats stopped working together as a matter of principle. The government kept having to shut down. Everybody watched the news but nobody quite trusted the news networks. People shouted at each other on social media and asked their friends to 'Like' it. When I review transcripts of online chats from those days, it's like eavesdropping on conversations from hell. They were rushing toward calamity and didn't seem to care."

I could see his point, partly. "All those factors probably paved the way for the war, but I don't see the value of setting the date so early."

"Real life isn't like that, Dak. We look back on it afterwards and try to place boundaries—it started here, it ended there. But life's messier than that. They were already hating each other on a massive scale long before the so-called war began. Once the hating started, they were in so deep they couldn't stop."

I thought about that a moment. The kid made sense.

Finally I sighed and said, "It does seem like they lost the ability to talk to each other. I've never understood why."

"I'll tell you," he said. "Because conservatives and liberals both became self-indulgent. They paid lip service to free speech and open discussion, but more and more they just put each other down. At first they were condescending and then they became hostile. I'm not just talking about politicians. The real problem started when the masses did it. With so many people on social media, everybody was so busy posturing, they were too busy to listen to each other. Finally it got to the point where they just couldn't get along anymore."

Woody went down the list: "Liberal against conservative, white against black, straight against gay, native against foreigner, male against female, blue collar against white collar, educated against uneducated…"

"It was all against all," L'Monjello said.

"What saved us?" Woody asked. "How did we pull out of the tail spin?"

L'Monjello smiled. "President LaShondra Jackson saved us, Woody. I don't think anybody else could've done it."

Woody nodded. We all knew the story. Ms. Jackson was the Vice President when that bomb blast killed the Chief Executive and his entourage. She almost died herself. The left half of her body was paralyzed for the rest of her life.

"She was a beautiful young woman before that," Woody said. "I remember those days."

"And yet I'll never forget the way she spoke from then on," I added. "That slur in her speech, the facial paralysis. They were constant reminders of the price she paid for our country. For all of us."

L'Monjello agreed. "She became the rallying point. For her sake, people stopped hating each other. Out of respect for her sacrifice, they found new respect for the office she held. And then they worked together to end the conflict."

"I was a little kid," I said. "I'll never forget the horror of it, or the deep love we all had for that woman."

"I was older," said Woody. "But I've spent a lifetime trying to forget."

L'Monjello was thoughtful. "It ended long before I was born, but it's always seemed like the elephant in the room. Nobody ever wants to talk about it. I worry that we might not have learned our lesson."

"And well you should, young man!"

It was the Professor. I had forgotten about him. He had gone off in a corner by himself, and I didn't think he was listening.

He came over and sat next to Woody. Facing L'Monjello, he continued. "For even you have failed to understand."

With his head raised heavenward, his eyes closed, he said, "We have never learned. And we *will* never learn."

He was quiet a moment, and then he looked around at us, one by one. He seemed weary.

"This thing we call 'civilization' is a fiction. We're not civilized. We never have been. We're brutes. We've always been at war, and we *will* be until the end. Someday we'll destroy ourselves. Then there will be peace on earth. Only then."

We looked around at each other uncomfortably.

He continued. "I've asked myself why I care. Why am I looking for Basil? Why not let the aliens destroy us? Wouldn't it be better that way?" He shook his head. "I don't know the answer to that. I only know that I must do what I can. But we don't deserve it."

He lifted his head dismally and said in a ghoulish voice:

"We... are an evil race!"

He held out the syllables:

Weeeeeeee
are an
Eee-viiiillll
Raaaaaaaaaaaaaacccce

The final consonant hung in the air as a hissing sound.

The rest of us glanced at each other. There was a long, awkward silence.

"Wow," L'Monjello said after awhile. "Talk about a conversation killer."

Woody glanced cautiously at the Professor out of the corner of his eye. "You're not religious, are you?"

The Professor was embarrassed by the question. "Pffft! No!" he said.

Apparently satisfied with that answer, Woody got up and walked away. But the Professor stared off into space and added, very quietly, "Not anymore."

18 THE BOTBALL MATCH

"Where's L'Monjello?" I asked, looking at my watch.

The others didn't know.

The game had already started. Robotic creatures of various sizes and shapes were chasing a ball around the field and trying to destroy each other at the same time. Metal clashed against metal. Bombs exploded. The crowd cheered. The play-by-play was deafening.

When we had left his apartment, L'Monjello wasn't ready to come with us. He was still on the phone making arrangements.

"Are you serious?" I told him. "You're the most important piece of this puzzle."

"I know, I know," he said. "Don't worry. I'll meet you there."

The three of us had looked at each other cautiously and gone on ahead without him. We moved the shuttle over to the stadium parking lot, got our tickets, and waited in the open-air stadium. Too nervous to sit, we paced along the sidelines on the home team side.

Now we were well into the game, and L'Monjello was still a no-show.

Woody and the Professor stood there listening to me complain. "He's the key to this whole thing. If he doesn't show up..."

The Professor took a step toward the playing field.

"Be careful, there!" I told him. "Do you know what happens if you take even one step onto the field during a Botball game?"

"No," he said absently. "What does it matter?"

"It's a war zone out there. If you don't watch your step, you can get hit by one of the contestants. And if nothing else, the referees may penalize the home team and the crowd will yell at you."

The Professor shuddered. "What a vulgar pastime!"

I knew I was losing my patience, but this was our only chance. If we didn't do it now, we might never do it at all. This was no time for L'Monjello to have cold feet.

I looked over at Brie's trailer with disgust. What a prima donna! She lived on campus, and yet she awaited her performance in a fancy trailer, like some celebrity.

I didn't dare tell L'Monjello, but I had done my homework the day before, and I expected the crowd to be rowdy during her performance. Although Brie was a hit among middle schoolers, she was mocked by her peers here at The Valley. I wondered why her producer had arranged for her to sing and dance in front of a hostile audience.

I turned to the Professor. "Are you absolutely sure we need L'Monjello for this?"

He scowled. "You know the answer to that."

There was a loud crash as a robot named Iron John brought down his prodigious ax on the head of a nearby opponent, splitting him in two. The jockey inside unbuckled his seatbelt and ran for his life.

"Good heavens!" cried the Professor. "What savagery!"

With a sigh of relief, I could see L'Monjello hurrying toward us. He had on a black leather jacket and dark glasses.

"It's about time," I told him. "What were you doing?"

He didn't answer me.

"Are you ready now?"

He nodded, and the two of us headed toward Brie's trailer. As L'Monjello had said, there were lots of crewmembers milling around, some of whom looked like thugs. Under his breath, L'Monjello pointed out Brie's PR person. She was wearing jeans and had bright purple hair that stood out straight at all angles.

For the first time since my arrival at The Valley, I took off my disguise. We hurried up to her.

"Tamra Taransky?" I asked.

She turned in my direction, then did a double-take.

"Dak Blayzak from the Global News Network."

She stared at me, entranced. "You're alive!" she said.

"Yes I am. But if I hear that one more time, I'm going to kill my publicist."

It took her a minute to recover, but then we got down to business. Yes, she said, she was associated with Brie, and yes, she'd be delighted to arrange an interview. When I asked if I could speak to Brie before the halftime show, she hurried to find her producer.

While we waited, a voice behind me said, "Hey, Dak!"

I turned around to find a student holding up his phone, taping me.

"It *is* you!" he said. "Wait'll my friends see this! What brings you to The Valley, Dak?"

I held up my hand and turned away. "Get rid of him," I said.

L'Monjello told him to move along. He stepped back a little but kept taping.

"Is he here to interview the Ice Princess?" the kid asked. "What a waste of time."

L'Monjello bristled. "Don't make me hurt you."

A middle-aged guy with curly black hair, wire rim glasses, and a Hawaiian shirt came bounding toward us.

"That's her uncle," L'Monjello whispered. "He runs the show."

"Well, well, well," said the uncle. "Wow! Dak Blayzak! Tamra says you want to interview Brie! Amazing!"

We just stood there.

"Sorry," he said, wiping his sweaty hand on his pants and extending it to me. "I'm Roi DiMarco, her producer. I'll be glad to let you talk to Brie—absolutely—but it'll have to be after the show. She's getting ready right now."

"I understand that," I told him, but I really wanted to find a way to make this happen now. "Can I ask you a few questions?"

I got him talking so I could have time to think about my next step. Meanwhile, in the background, Tamra rushed out of Brie's trailer with a look of panic on her face. She hurried to some of her staff members, who shook their heads and ran in opposite directions.

"Something's wrong," I said over my shoulder, but there was no response. I looked all around. L'Monjello was gone.

A staff member joined us and whispered something to Roi. "Excuse me, Dak," he said. "I'll be back in a moment." And he hurried away with the staffer.

I rushed to the Professor and Woody. "Brie's missing!" I announced.

"No she's not," they told me. "She's right there." And they pointed toward the playing field.

My jaw dropped. Just as they said, she was running nimbly between the metallic combatants, with projectiles narrowly missing her on either side.

"She could die out there!" I said.

Woody looked startled. "I assumed it was part of the show."

Brie's people were on the sidelines, trying to call her back. Uncle Roi was shouting over a microphone, demanding that the game stop immediately. A chant came up from the crowd: "Don't stop! Don't stop!"

One of the machines reached out with a tentacle and caught her in a pincer grip. The crowd cheered as it carried her over to the sidelines. But as it released her, she held onto it, climbing up the tentacle and onto the machine.

"What's she doing?" Woody asked.

I shook my head. "I don't get it."

She sat perched on top of the robot and, looking very somber, slowly unfurled a handwritten banner.

It said, "HELP ME."

19 THE GETAWAY

The crowd grew silent. Even the play-by-play stopped.

The three of us were stunned.

Oblivious to what was happening, the jockeys still piloted their robots around the field and continued to try to destroy each other. One smashed into the robot Brie was riding and she lost her balance. The banner fell from her hands and she almost tumbled onto the field.

A girl shouted, "Somebody help her!"

People got up from the stands and started toward the field, but it was too dangerous. Unaware of what was happening, the jockeys were still shooting at each other. One of the machines had a spinning metal arm that almost hit Brie as it passed.

All over the stadium, people were shouting. "Help her! Stop the game!"

"Where's Mr. Parker?" the Professor asked.

Suddenly the crowd cheered and Woody pointed toward the far end of the field. "There!"

L'Monjello was racing above the playing field on a flying motorcycle.

Slowing down, he hovered beside Brie and gestured to her. After a moment's hesitation, she jumped on behind him and held onto his leather jacket. Then they flew over our heads and out of the arena. The whole stadium was on its feet, roaring its approval.

I sprinted to the nearest exit, with Woody and the Professor struggling to keep up. Once out of the stadium, I could see some of Uncle Roi's thugs ahead of us, jumping into various kinds of hovercraft and racing after L'Monjello.

Still running, I reached into my pocket for the shuttle's remote control. The engine started, the doors slowly opened, and the ramp lowered just in time for me to run up it.

"Hurry!" I told the others. "We've got to catch up with them!"

The kid with the cell phone was in the distance, still taping.

As soon as Woody and the Professor boarded the shuttle, it took off. We could see L'Monjello and Brie flying into a forest with Uncle Roi's men right behind them. There was a ravine, and L'Monjello flew low over it. There were trees on the banks of the ravine, and L'Monjello weaved in and out of them, trying to elude his captors. Their vehicles weren't easy to maneuver, and they almost collided with each other as they tried to avoid hitting the trees.

A voice came over the shuttle intercom. "Woody! Are you there?"

"That's L'Monjello!" Woody said. "How do I answer him?"

All three of us searched the control panel.

"Dak!" the voice said. "Professor! Can anybody hear me?"

Finally Woody found the right switch. "L'Monjello, it's Woody!"

"Thank God!" he said. "Do you know where the Campus Center is?"

"Is that the one with the circular drive out front?"

"Right! Park out front and leave the door open. I'll meet you there!"

On our instructions, the shuttle stopped pursuing L'Monjello and flew south, over the tops of buildings.

"Look!" Woody said.

Behind the Campus Center, there was a hillside descending toward a big pond. It was a gathering place for students, but today it looked like a motorcycle convention.

"There must be over a hundred bikes down there," I said.

Every rider had a black leather jacket and dark glasses. And all of them were revving their engines.

We flew around to the front of the Campus Center and landed in the circular drive. Immediately we were surrounded by motorcycles. As the door of the shuttle opened and we stepped out, some students hurried toward us. "We're friends of L'Monjello. He wants you to stay in the shuttle and be ready to take off."

We got back in but kept the door open.

"Hey, Dak!" It was the kid with the cell phone. He had just arrived on his bicycle and was trying to come into the shuttle, but the students outside stopped him.

Suddenly L'Monjello's cycle came flying from behind one of the buildings and skimmed over the top of the pond. A cheer went up from the crowd, echoing off the nearby buildings. Brie's bodyguards appeared next around the corner, but it was too late. L'Monjello had already landed among the hundreds of other cycles, and his friends had surrounded him.

Woody filled us in. "There's a back entrance to the Campus Center down by the pond. If they go in that way and climb a flight of stairs, they'll be up here soon."

A few minutes later, L'Monjello and Brie came running out of the Campus Center toward the shuttle.

"Let's go!" L'Monjello said as they ran up the ramp.

The door closed and the shuttle took flight immediately. Looking back, we could see Brie's bodyguards scanning the crowd of motorcycles, unsure what to do next. While they hesitated, the cycles began flying away in all directions. The thugs looked totally confused.

But the kid with the cell phone was watching us fly away, and he was still taping.

When our shuttle's steep climb was over, L'Monjello opened a drawer and pulled out a woman's sweat suit. "Here," he told Brie. "I thought you might be more relaxed in this. There's a changing room in the back. I hope it fits."

She stared at it. "I never get to dress casually." Then she looked up at him. "That's so thoughtful of you."

He kept holding it out to her, and finally she accepted it. "Thank you. I'll be right back."

We all tried to question him at once, but he shook his head. "I don't want her to hear us whispering about her."

It didn't take her long to change. When she rejoined us, her hair was tied in the back, and she looked a lot more comfortable. Sitting across from L'Monjello and observing him a moment, she seemed awe-struck. "You're L'Monjello Parker, aren't you?"

"You know me?"

"I've wanted to meet you since I moved here," she said. "All the real students talk about you."

"Aren't you a real student?"

She looked disappointed. "Let's not lie to each other, please. Nobody's ever honest with me."

He had regretted saying it as soon as it left his lips. "Okay," he said. "Sorry."

They sat there a moment, and he tried again. "Can I ask you something?"

She nodded.

"What were you doing out there on the field? You could've been hurt."

She looked around at us, then back at him. "Don't you know?"

He shook his head.

"But you were right there, ready to help! I thought you knew."

L'Monjello didn't say anything.

"I was trying to escape," she said. "My Uncle Roi has been holding me captive for years."

20 INTERNET PHENOMENON

"I couldn't take it anymore," Brie said. "I've tried to escape many times, but they always catch me. I decided this would be the last time. I'd either succeed... or die trying."

L'Monjello was shocked. "Brie," he said, "I've watched your show every day for the past two years. If I had only known!"

She shook her head. "Nobody knew. Uncle Roi made sure of that. He never let me near anyone who might be sympathetic."

Her mother had died when she was very little, and her maternal grandmother had taken her in. "She was kind," she said, "but my Uncle Roi took advantage of her. Anything he wanted, he got. He gambled and piled up debts of one sort or another, and she always bailed him out. He kept talking about earning a fortune someday, and he always had some scheme going. None of them ever panned out, but Grandma paid for them all.

"As I started to grow up, he kept looking at me..."

"Did he—"

"No, he never touched me. I can be glad of that much. But he looked at me a lot, and when he thought I wasn't listening, he told Grandma that I could earn them all a fortune.

"For once he was right. I did."

Her grandmother gave Roi permission to turn her into a celebrity. At first, she had found it somewhat exciting, but he never consulted her. He made her take voice lessons, guitar lessons, dancing lessons—none of which she ever remembered wanting to do. Meanwhile, she rarely got to do the things that mattered most to her.

"Sometimes," she said, "I just wanted to sit down with a good book or have a few friends over. More and more, Uncle Roi started taking over my life, telling me what I could and couldn't do, and choosing my friends for me."

With her grandmother's blessing and financial backing, her uncle set up a Home Channel. Brie was on the Internet about a year before the show went viral. After that, brand-name companies came knocking on Uncle Roi's door proposing sponsorships, and the money started pouring in. Her uncle used some of the funds to make the show more glitzy. Soon there were story developers and scriptwriters. None of her co-stars were real people after that. They were all actors. And none of them were friendly.

"Uncle Roi was careful to surround me with people who would carry out *his* wishes—not mine. They weren't just showbiz people; they were spies. I didn't realize that at first, and I spoke too freely. Everything I said got back to him, and sometimes I was punished."

She never got to experience high school except through role-playing. "Everything was make-believe: my school, my classes, my so-called friends—they were all fake. I was a cheerleader for a team that didn't exist. My first kiss—"

She shuddered. "Everything was staged."

Her grandmother died during Brie's high school years. She had put her part of the show's earnings into a trust fund for Brie, but she had unwisely appointed her son as trustee. Brie never saw any of that money.

Her first escape attempt was just after her grandmother died. The spies were onto her before she even got out the door.

She thought long and hard before her next try. This time she believed she could pull it off. She was signing autographs at a mall to celebrate the release of her first album, and she was surrounded by her uncle's thugs. A sweet-looking old lady bought a CD for her grandchild, and Brie wrote beneath her autograph, "I'm being held against my will. Please tell the authorities."

The old lady took a few steps, read the note, and went straight to her uncle.

"I couldn't believe it," Brie said. "The old lady asked him, 'What'll you pay me to keep quiet about this?' Then she turned and looked at me like I was a winning lottery ticket."

There were other attempts, but each time she was punished, and with each failure she became less hopeful.

"Then Uncle Roi told me something I never expected to hear. Just after my fake graduation, he sat down with me and told me I was going to The Valley in the fall.

"'Wait,' I said. 'A real college?'

"'That's right,' he said. 'Can I trust you, Brie? Will you stop trying to escape?'

"'Absolutely!' I said. 'This is great! I never thought I'd get to go to a real college!'

"I thanked him over and over—I even hugged him! It never dawned on me that he'd confine me to a soundstage once we got on campus. We were at a real school, but my life was still fake.

"That's when I decided to take matters into my own hands. If I couldn't escape, I'd have to find other ways to get what I wanted. I knew he would never give me an ounce of freedom as long as I was earning him money, so I did what I could to sabotage the show. I messed up my lines on purpose. I read them as unconvincingly as I could. He knew what I was up to, and he punished me, but I refused to cooperate with him. Sometimes I'd make up lines just to throw off the other actors. They'd all get mad at me and start making up lines of their own, then Uncle Roi would get mad at *them*."

She turned to L'Monjello. "Some of the extras and stagehands were Valley students. I liked to eavesdrop. They often mentioned you... how smart you were, and how kind... and I thought to myself, *Never in a million years will I get to meet someone like that.*

"Meanwhile, I plotted my escape. This time I was patient. It took a lot of persuading, but I convinced Uncle Roi to let me do this halftime show today. I knew that my only hope of escape would be at a public event. If I could just get in front of a live audience and plead with them to help me...

"But a Botball match was the perfect event. Even if no one cared, maybe I could be injured—"

"Brie!"

"—and hospitalized, and maybe they'd finally listen. Or maybe I'd die, and that would be okay too."

Unable to bear another word of it, L'Monjello reached out to her, and she took his hand in both of hers.

"I just hoped somebody would do something," she said. "I never thought it would be you."

He shook his head. "If I had known, I would've come sooner."

"You were there," she said. "That's what matters."

They sat looking into each other's eyes, and Brie held tightly onto his hand.

"How did you get through it?" he asked. "How did you find the strength to keep going?"

She looked down at his hand and thought for a moment. "I've never told anybody this. The one bright spot, all through the years, has been the thought of my mother. She died in a car crash when I was six. I only have a few memories of her, but they were enough to sustain me. My favorite one was of bedtime. She'd rock me and stroke my hair and whisper, 'My beautiful Cambria.'"

"Cambria?"

"That's my real name. Uncle Roi shortened it."

She looked off into space, remembering. "When my mother spoke, it was like music. 'My beautiful Cambria,' she'd say, and it sounded like a song. I felt so safe and happy in those arms. All my life, whenever I've reached my limit and just couldn't go on another day, I've imagined myself back there... drifting off to sleep... listening to her wonderful voice..."

21 WE'VE LOST HER

The shuttle landed in a secluded forest. Brie hurried out to look at the tall pine trees and inhale the air.

"Freedom!" she said. She shouted it again, just to hear it echo. Then she laughed. "I can't believe this is really happening."

She pulled L'Monjello toward her and kissed him.

"Thank you!" she said. "Thanks for being there when I needed you!"

Plop!

They looked down to find a burlap sack at their feet and the Professor standing beside them, waiting.

"What's that?" she asked.

L'Monjello sighed. Taking her hand in his, he said, "We have to talk."

For a while they strolled hand-in-hand. L'Monjello gestured and shrugged as Brie listened intently. Then she stopped and pulled away from him. He approached her and she pushed him. She hurried back to the Professor.

"I'm not playing your game," she told him. "I don't want any part of this!"

"She thinks the Communicator will tell her to go back," L'Monjello explained.

"Of course it will!" she said. "I don't know anybody outside the show. Uncle Roi shielded me from people my whole life."

"You don't know what it'll say," L'Monjello told her.

"Sure I do. If all the people in my life are associated with the show in some way, it doesn't matter which one gets picked. You're telling me I have to go back."

"No, we're not."

She pointed at the burlap sack. "That thing is."

He reached out to her and she moved away.

"Listen to me," he said. "*That thing* read my mind. I don't know how, but it did. It told me to take the biggest risk of my life. It told me to reach out to the person I wanted to meet most in the whole world. You."

She looked like her resolve was melting for a moment, but then she shook her head. "I can't imagine how something like that could possibly happen to me."

"I'm just saying that the Communicator wanted what was best for me—and for you! I don't know how or even why that's the case, but it's true. I can't believe it will ask you to go back."

Woody and I looked at each other. It sounded like L'Monjello was a believer now. But did he honestly think that the aliens cared about Brie's happiness?

I glanced over at the Professor, sure that he'd be disgusted with the way the conversation was going, but instead I saw him nodding.

Brie looked dismal. "I need to take a walk," she said. "Alone." And she started back toward the forest.

None of us wanted to let her go. L'Monjello called after her.

"Brie…"

She stopped to listen, but kept her back to us and her head bowed.

"Take as long as you need. Just remember this. No matter what the Communicator says, I won't let anyone take you captive again."

When he finished, she nodded. Then she walked away into the forest.

He sighed. "I've lost her."

"We all have," said the Professor.

Woody gave each of us a look of disapproval. "Am I the only optimist in this group?"

We thought about that for a half-second and said, in unison, "Yes."

It seemed like ages, but half an hour later she slowly came back from the forest.

"I can't believe you let me go," she said.

We remained silent.

"That means a lot," she told us. "I wasn't planning on coming back."

"We assumed that," I said.

She looked surprised. "And you let me go anyway?"

The Professor sighed and pointed at L'Monjello. "We left it up to him."

She approached L'Monjello and looked like she was going to kiss him again, but there wasn't time for that.

The Professor took the Communicator out of the burlap sack and held it out to her. "Place one hand on each end and I will read it."

She turned to L'Monjello.

He nodded. "I won't let them take you away."

With a look of resignation, she held onto the Communicator. An image appeared on the screen.

The Professor read the monitor gravely and said nothing.

"Who is it?" she asked. "It's my Uncle Roi, isn't it?"

"No," he replied.

"Someone else from the show?"

"No."

"Then—"

The Professor was deeply troubled. "It's worse."

He turned away and gazed heavenward. "How can this be right?" he whispered.

"What is it?" she asked.

He stared at her a moment. "The aliens want you to contact your mother."

22 MISSING PERSON

As an investigative journalist, I've had a little practice finding missing persons. So it didn't take me long to locate Brie's mother online.

Her name was Monica DiMarco, and she was alive. There had been no car crash.

"They lied to me!" Brie said. "Grandma... Uncle Roi. They both lied to me!"

For the past fifteen years—most of Brie's life—Monica had been living in a prison in Ankara, Turkey.

"She was a criminal?"

Nobody said anything.

"What was the charge?"

"It's restricted," I told her. "Every time I find something about it online, it stops me and says it's classified."

"Was she a spy?"

"I'm not sure of anything," I said.

She turned away, and with her back to us, she said, "You think you know a person. I was so little, but I trusted her. She was my world. My refuge. Through all the intervening years, she was my one ray of hope. And now..."

L'Monjello spoke softly. "We don't know enough to judge, Brie."

She thought about that a moment, then shook her head. "I don't care if she had reasons for what she did. We all have reasons for the things we do. But she wasn't there for me... because of something she did... something so bad that we're not supposed to know."

Her face was red. "Did she ever think of me? Did she ever stop to think that I needed her?"

I glanced at the Professor and he looked back at me, deeply grieved.

We both knew what had to happen next, but neither of us wanted to say it.

She noticed. "Don't worry, Professor. I understand what I have to do. I won't like it, but I'll do it." She turned to me. "Is she still in prison?"

"No," I said. "She was released a few months ago."

"Really! And she didn't even bother to look me up."

Again, nobody answered her.

"Okay, then. If she doesn't want to be part of my life, then this should be an easy job. In and out. Hand over the Communicator and I'm done. Right?"

She looked at the Professor, but he said nothing.

"I don't see any reason why I have to stick around after that. This is kind of a relay race, isn't it? I do my part and I'm done?"

The Professor sighed. "It doesn't work that way. We're all in this until we find Basil."

"Are you sure? Is that in the by-laws?"

"It's just... something I sense."

"Well... I'll do whatever I can to help. But I'm not going to spend any time with that woman."

The Professor turned to me. "Where's she living?"

"In St. Louis," I said. "We can be there in a couple of hours."

Brie walked up the ramp of the shuttle. "Let's go then... and get this over with."

During the flight to St. Louis, L'Monjello and Brie had a long heart-to-heart talk, huddled together in a two-person seat in a corner of the shuttle. I heard her voice most of the time, but once in a while his gentle bass would answer her reassuringly. I glanced over once and saw her head resting on his shoulder.

The Professor sat in a window seat, staring intently into the sky.

Woody seemed bored. He made a quick phone call to his wife, then just fidgeted. He kept looking over at me, but I ignored him.

This was the first block of time I had had to start taking notes for my book. Over the past few days, I had become convinced that this story couldn't be reduced to a news brief or even a series of reports. As the events unfolded, I started mapping them out in my head, trying to figure out how to organize them in written form.

I had always wanted to write a book about my experiences as a journalist, but this story seemed to cry out for literary expression.

So now, as I sat alone and hurriedly typed up everything I could think of into the Notes app on the shuttle's computer—bits and pieces of dialogue, facial expressions, my thoughts about each of these people—it all started to come together. Even if the Professor was crazy and Basil was a mere phantom, I would still come out ahead, because I could write a book about this strange odyssey.

I typed furiously, chuckling at times.

I've always loved doing television journalism, but it had been good for me to spend some time away from Naif. In the past few days, something had been awakened within me. I realized that I had come to rely much too heavily on the camera to tell my stories for me. Suddenly I was forced to pay attention to sights and sounds and to express them in words. It was deeply satisfying, unlike anything I had ever done before.

Woody appeared at my side, trying to read what was on my screen. "What are you doing, Dak?"

Startled, I turned the computer off and put it away. "Nothing."

"Hmm," he said suspiciously. "Why didn't you want me to see it?"

Irritated, I got up and walked to the back of the shuttle. On a whim, I decided to check my messages on my phone. There were hundreds of them, many from Maggie, my personal assistant, and many others from Naif. I decided to Skype Naif.

He looked frantic. "Where the hell are you?"

I smirked. "Look, Naif—"

"This isn't funny, Dak. Every journalist in the country is searching for you. You're the top story right now, and I'm out of the loop."

"What are you talking about?"

"People think you're dead."

"Huh? Why?"

"The Juliet, remember? They saw you die while the clones were fighting."

"Naif, didn't you edit that out?"

"I don't have time to argue with you. Everybody thinks you're dead and GNN's covering it up. The other networks don't believe it, of course, but they think you're onto something big and they're determined to find you. And I'm here twiddling my thumbs."

I had to sit down.

"What's with the secrecy?" he asked. "Why can't you tell me where you are?"

"Sorry," I said. "Not yet."

"Do you want Fru Phillips to find you before I do?"

The veins in my neck tightened. Naif knew just how to get me riled up.

"There's something else," he said. "It's about the clones."

I cocked my head. "What about them?"

"Several of them are here. They're looking for you."

"Why?"

"They think you're in danger. They've come to rescue you."

"Oh, good grief!"

"You freed them. They want to return the favor. And you know how resourceful they are. They'll find you. And Fru will be right behind them."

I sighed. "Is there anything else I should know?"

"That depends. There's another video out there. Some kid with a cell phone. Is it true you kidnapped that girl?"

I didn't answer him.

"Dak! Tell me you had nothing to do with that!"

"Uh, Naif—"

"Well guess what. Her uncle has 'people'—you know what I mean? Guys with weapons. Thugs, Dak. And they're coming for the girl. Why don't you tell me where you are?"

This was getting out of hand. I thought about it a moment, then shook my head. "If I told you, they'd all follow you straight to me. Sorry, pal."

Naif was so mad, none of his words came out right. I saved him the trouble and hung up.

23 REUNION

It was dark by the time our shuttle descended into St. Louis, but we could see that it wasn't the best of neighborhoods. There were lots of boarded-up storefronts and ramshackle houses. We landed in front of a decrepit-looking two-story house.

Monica DiMarco rented the upper floor. Along the side of the house, there were stairs leading up to her apartment. The wood was old and rickety, and some of the steps had already broken through.

L'Monjello and Brie started toward the shuttle exit, and he turned to the rest of us. "We think it's best for us to go up together first. The rest of you stay here, and we'll tell you when we're ready."

We agreed, and through the windows of the shuttle we watched them take cautious steps upward. The staircase swayed back and forth as they ascended.

Brie knocked, and L'Monjello stood close behind her.

After a moment, the door opened slowly. I couldn't see who was on the other side of it, nor could I hear what was said, but Brie's face was stern as she spoke. There was a moment's hesitation, then she looked up at L'Monjello. He said something, and they stepped inside.

"Do you think they'll be safe?" Woody asked.

"Well, they've just knocked on the door of an ex-convict. She may have a bunch of her sleazy friends up there with her..."

"Let's go," he said, and he stormed out of the shuttle.

"Professor?"

"After you, Mr. Blayzak."

We locked up the shuttle and stood at the foot of the stairs. Woody wanted to go up, but as we hesitated before the treacherous staircase, L'Monjello came out and waved for us to come. I still don't know how we made it up those stairs without the whole thing collapsing under our feet.

L'Monjello stopped the Professor in the doorway. "I need to see the Communicator."

He tried to pass, but the young man insisted.

With great reluctance, the Professor handed him the burlap sack. L'Monjello reached in and felt around a moment. Then he gave it back.

We entered the apartment and stood in a little kitchen. It had a small stove and a table with a single chair. Beyond the kitchen was a small sitting room with a dim lamp. The sofa had stuffing sticking out of it at several spots. There were no sleazy characters in sight, other than the one we had come to visit.

We all stood in a circle in the sitting room. Nobody wanted to sit on that couch.

Brie introduced her mother to us with unconcealed disgust. She was an emaciated woman, middle-aged, with dark unwashed hair, shoulder length, and deep-set, brooding eyes. She wore a tattered t-shirt and jeans. There were scars on both of her arms. She expressed no interest in any of us.

After the introductions, Brie turned to the Professor and said, "I have explained what we're here to do, and Monica has agreed to cooperate."

I glanced at the woman to see how she liked hearing her daughter refer to her as "Monica," but she showed no emotion.

Surprisingly, the Professor took pity on the woman. He pulled the Communicator slowly out of the burlap sack and handed it to her. In a gentle voice, he said, "Take it in both of your hands, my dear, and I'll do the rest."

She did as she was told, again without emotion.

The Professor studied the device a moment, then searched her face earnestly. "The Communicator is asking you to contact someone," he said. "The description of that person is in two parts." He read the monitor again and said, "One who makes the truth a lie…"

Now, for the first time, she showed emotion. She shut her eyes and bowed her head as if she were in agony. The Professor continued.

"…the one who has the All-Seeing Eye."

Woody laughed. "Hey, that rhymes!"

Monica whirled around and glared at him, then at all of us. "You people have no idea what you've gotten yourselves into! You act like a bunch of tourists! You wouldn't last one minute in there!"

The Professor tried to take the Communicator from her, but she grabbed the burlap sack out of his hands and put the device inside it herself. "I'm going alone," she said.

Everyone protested at once.

"It's not up for debate," she told us. "Where I'm going, none of you belong." Holding up the burlap sack, she added, "I'm taking this with me."

"But who will read it?" the Professor asked.

"Leave that to me," she said.

There was general confusion as all of us tried to talk sense into her, but her mind was made up. "You can stay here until I get back," she told us. "You'll be safer here."

She was on her way out the door when she stopped suddenly, thought a moment, then turned around. Hurrying back to L'Monjello, she gripped his hand tightly.

"Promise me you'll take care of my daughter," she said.

I was surprised at the look L'Monjello gave her. It was like they had a special understanding, like something had clicked between them and they knew more about each other than words could tell.

He fixed his eyes upon her and said, very gravely, "I will!"

She nodded, then turned and marched out the door without another word.

Brie stomped over to him. "What right do you have to tell—that woman—you'll take care of me! I've done just fine all these years without her—and you!"

He sat down at the little the kitchen table and took out his phone. "What was I supposed to do—refuse? You saw how she was."

Brie turned away muttering to herself, and the Professor fell onto the couch with his head in his hands. "I can't believe what I just did! I let an ex-convict walk away with my Communicator and disappear into the night!"

"Relax," L'Monjello told him. "I'm on it."

"What do you mean?"

The young man held up his phone. "I attached a GPS to the Communicator. I'm tracking her right now."

24 WHO IS THIS WOMAN?

Monica walked several blocks, then a vehicle picked her up. We saw it on the GPS. She was just a throbbing yellow dot on the screen, but suddenly the dot raced forward.

"Let's go," L'Monjello said, and we headed back to the shuttle.

Once inside, he hooked up his phone to the overhead TV, and we sat watching the yellow dot.

It sped across town, turning in at a small airstrip.

"That's a military base," I said. "What's her connection there?"

L'Monjello typed in a command, and, using a satellite, we were able to get a real-time aerial view of her. She was in a black limousine, and it drove out onto the airstrip and stopped. A soldier came forward and opened the door for her, saluting as she stepped out. She touched her forehead in response. Reaching back inside the limousine, she pulled out the Professor's burlap sack and strung it over her shoulder. After looking around for a moment, she boarded a private jet.

"Who *is* this woman?" Woody asked.

The jet took off and, on L'Monjello's command, our shuttle took flight as well.

"I don't know," he said, "But wherever *she's* going, *we're* going."

Of course, we couldn't match her speed, but we could follow her, at least. Switching off satellite mode, we sat mesmerized, watching the blinking yellow dot move westward.

"There is so much we don't know about her," Brie said at one point. "She could be leading us straight into hell."

The Professor nodded. "It's my understanding that that is exactly where she's going."

"And yet we're following her."

He nodded again. "Because we must."

It was a long trip. On through the night, we trailed her across Missouri, then Kansas, and into Colorado. She crossed the Rocky Mountains, turning slightly south. Somewhere in Nevada, she landed.

"What's around there?" I asked.

L'Monjello shook his head. "Nothing. She's in the middle of a desert."

He tried to view her by satellite, but access was denied.

Then the yellow dot disappeared.

Nobody said anything. We just kept going.

It took us an extra hour to arrive at the area where we had last seen the yellow dot, and as we got closer, we flew at a lower altitude. An alarm sounded.

"This area is off-limits," a male voice warned over the shuttle intercom. "Do not proceed."

We all looked at each other, but nobody said anything about turning back.

The voice repeated its warning and was again ignored.

I approached the console, with Woody close behind. "Any way to speed this thing up?" I asked.

We heard a thunderous roar. Above and around us were military helicopters.

"You have entered a restricted area," the voice said over the shuttle intercom. "You will stop and prepare to be boarded."

Woody pointed at the console. "They've taken control."

Our shuttle slowed down abruptly, then landed in the sand. The choppers hovered all around us. Soldiers jumped out of them and surrounded our vehicle, aiming laser rifles at us. L'Monjello moved in front of Brie as our shuttle door opened and two soldiers stood on either side of the ramp.

Then a man I knew very well walked through the door.

It was The Guy. And the soldiers were The Cavalry.

Only this time, they weren't here to help.

25 UNDER ARREST

The Guy said nothing. With one of his soldiers close behind, he entered the shuttle and looked around. His eyes didn't rest on any of us. He seemed to be checking the place out, making sure we didn't have weapons.

When he was satisfied, he stepped back down the ramp and spoke quietly to his men. Then he turned to the one who had been shadowing him and said, "You're with me, Donovan."

The other soldiers returned to their choppers and flew on ahead as The Guy and his assistant reboarded our shuttle, closing the door behind them. Donovan went to the controls and pushed a few buttons. Soon we were airborne, following the choppers across the desert.

"Are you going to tell us what's happening?" the Professor asked.

The Guy looked him over. "You're all under arrest, Professor. This area is restricted. You knew that."

L'Monjello's voice was calm. "We're looking for a friend of ours. We believe she's in danger. We came to help."

With a strange expression on his face, The Guy walked right up to L'Monjello and stood nose-to-nose with him. "A *friend* of yours?"

L'Monjello's eyes were defiant. "You heard right."

They stared each other down for a moment, and then The Guy turned away and drawled, "You've just told me everything I need to know about you, Mr. Parker."

"You know our names," said Woody.

"Yes, Mr. Wilson. We know your names. We've been expecting you."

The Guy walked over to me. "But I've known one of you for a long time."

89

"And yet," I said, "I have no idea who you are."

"My name's Gage," he told me. "And you've really done it this time, Dak. I can't get you out of this one."

We all sat down when Gage told us we'd be traveling for awhile. I noticed that we were coasting, as if he wasn't in a hurry to get us to our destination.

Turning to me, he said, "You never asked me who I work for."

"I always assumed it was the CIA."

"I know," he said. "And that was fine with me. The less you knew, the better."

"You're with the government, though, right?"

He shook his head. "The government isn't in charge anymore, Dak. Not ours or anybody else's. It's the multinational corporations that run things now. I work for one of them, although you don't need to know which one. I'm a small part of something called the Scenarios Division."

He pushed a button on a control panel near him and the TV monitor turned on.

"The mission of the Scenarios Division is to imagine possible futures for the world, and to make sure we end up with the right one."

Woody made a face. "You engineer happy endings?"

Donovan turned around and caught Gage's eye.

"Well," said Gage, "I guess that depends on which side you're on, Mr. Wilson."

He pushed a couple of other buttons and a sprawling organizational chart filled the TV monitor. "The Corporation divides the world into geographical areas. For each area, teams of social scientists report on what's happening. They chart out the main trends—economic, social, political. They pass that information on to a team of futurists, who work out alternative trajectories. After that, a team of writers turns those trends into open-ended stories."

"For what purpose?" I asked.

"In the beginning, we used to send focus groups out among the nations, share our different scenarios with them, and ask them to choose the future that sounded best to them. We did that in South Africa during the days of apartheid, for example."

"Wait a minute," said L'Monjello. "Why would multinational corporations spend all that time and money to help communities imagine 'possible futures'?"

"It was good for business," Gage said. "The last thing The

Corporation wanted was war... or any other kind of social upheaval. It's too costly. So they invested time and money in helping the locals think up better solutions to their problems."

"That all sounds fairly innocuous," I said. "But I get the impression that the system doesn't work like that anymore."

He pushed another button and items moved around on the org chart. "There have been some changes over the years. The first of these was a shift away from focus groups and local buy-in. *The Corporation* began making decisions instead. *They* decided how they wanted the story to end. And then they made sure things worked out the way they chose."

"Big difference," said Woody.

"But even then, the decision was made by more than one person. It was a special committee called The Board. For a number of years, they were pretty solid. Lots of wisdom in that group. I enjoyed working for them."

I interrupted. "You never told us what you do."

He zeroed in on a section of the chart. "I lead a unit of Catalysts. The facts have been gathered in, the alternative scenarios have been written, and The Board has made its decision. At that point, they send out a team of Catalysts to make sure the story plays out the way it's supposed to."

"According to The Board, you mean."

"Yes, according to The Board," said Gage. "Except... The Board no longer exists."

This time he punched the button angrily, and they disappeared from the chart.

"Who makes the decisions now?" I asked.

He snarled. "The one with the All-Seeing Eye."

All of us sat up. "What does that mean?"

"The All-Seeing Eye? It's a processing unit."

"A computer?"

"Yes, but a very special one. It takes all the information on the Internet, processes it, and presents it in a form that the human mind can grasp: it puts it all in story form."

L'Monjello was skeptical. "All the information in the world? That's impossible. There's way too much."

Gage nodded. "You're right, Mr. Parker. And, to complicate matters, the All-Seeing Eye has access to even more data than you or I will ever see: classified government information, medical records, therapists' notes, coroners' reports, student records—"

L'Monjello stopped him. "So how can it take all that information and make it digestible?"

"It's highly selective. Whoever has the All-Seeing Eye doesn't really know everything. Not even close. But they see a whole lot more than you and I ever will. The whole thing is driven by the wearer of the Eye. That person asks questions, and the computer answers them in story form. It all depends on what the wearer wants to know."

The Professor had been quiet through all of this, but now he spoke up. "It sounds like the person operating it would be tempted to think that he was omniscient."

"And omnipotent," Gage said. "But it's not true. Bear in mind that the All-Seeing Eye doesn't actually 'see' anything unless it's uploaded to the Internet. It can't see us having this conversation right now, for example. It can only see what people put onto the web. Now, of course, that's still plenty. Your datebook, your notes, your videos—anything you upload becomes fair game."

My curiosity was building. "You said there used to be a Board making decisions, but now that Board has been replaced by the one who has the All-Seeing Eye."

"Yes," he said with disgust. "My boss."

Brie's voice trembled slightly. "Who *is* that person, Mr. Gage?"

He turned to Brie with a look of deep sympathy. "Her name is Vera. And she and your mother used to be best friends."

26 A VERY STRANGE SCENARIO

"Did you know my mother?"

"Yes, ma'am," he said, and his voice was tender. "*She* used to be a Catalyst, too. The last of the great ones. She trained me."

Brie looked like she wanted to ask another question but decided not to.

"The name 'Monica DiMarco' used to command respect in our division," Gage said. "She had an amazing gift. Although she had troops under her command, she only used force as a last resort. She'd walk into the most dangerous situations and convince people to do the right thing."

"How?" we asked.

"By listening to them. She did her homework first: stayed up late nights, reading all the scenarios, trying to understand all sides. Then she'd go into a scene of conflict and get them talking to each other. It was quite a sight." He sighed. "I've always felt that *that's* what a Catalyst should do. But things changed after Vera took over."

Vera was a Catalyst who liked shortcuts. "Knowledge is power," she used to say, but she didn't have the patience to read all the scenarios. "There has to be a way to download all this information," she said.

A team of Corporation scientists agreed. They offered her The All-Seeing Eye.

"This device," they promised her, "will give you access to all that's happening—everywhere, 24/7. The experience of the whole human race will be distilled and downloaded for your consumption."

Vera had laughed at that. "Sounds like an updated version of the forbidden fruit." But she was keenly interested. "Knowledge *is* power," she said.

There was just one catch. To make room for the implant, she would have to give up one of her own eyes.

"And she agreed to that?" Woody said.

Gage nodded. "In exchange for a window to the world? Absolutely, Mr. Wilson. She found it irresistible. All of us who knew her tried to talk her out of it. Monica protested more loudly than the rest of us. But Vera wouldn't listen. Only after she had had the surgery did she realize that there was another catch... and then it was too late."

"Something the scientists didn't tell her?" I asked.

"Something they didn't foresee. Nobody saw it coming. When Vera woke up from her surgery and started using the device, she just sobbed uncontrollably. She reported being overwhelmed."

L'Monjello cut in. "Just like I said. Too much information."

"No, the All-Seeing Eye took care of that. The data it fed her was already digested. No, Mr. Parker, for the first time ever, a human being was allowed to peer into the private lives of people everywhere and share their experiences firsthand. And to her great surprise—and the surprise of the team of scientists—she was overwhelmed by the suffering in the world. It wasn't *information* overload; it was *emotional* overload. Suddenly, she felt the pain of the whole world, and she couldn't bear it.

"The neurologists discussed a number of solutions, but none of them were workable. The wires in the box had so thoroughly fused with her brain tissue, they couldn't remove it without causing serious damage. And at any rate, there was no way to put her back together again cosmetically. You'll see what I mean. So they did nothing... and she screamed and cried until she couldn't take it anymore. At that point, her brain shut down. She went into a self-induced coma.

"It lasted a few days. But when she came out of it, she had a new personality. Somehow, she had turned off her emotions. Since that day, she's never had the slightest bit of sympathy for anybody. That was the first thing we noticed. It took us a while to discover the other thing."

"The other thing" was a new sense of resolve. From now on, she would do something about the world's problems.

Using her inside knowledge, she blackmailed members of The Board and got them to turn over their power to her. Those who couldn't be coerced died mysteriously. Within a matter of weeks, Vera went from being just one of many Catalysts to being the Supreme Commander of the Scenarios Division. And with her newly-acquired power, she set out to right the world's wrongs—as she saw them.

"Bear in mind," Gage said, "she no longer had sympathy for anybody. So now the world's problems seemed much more cut-and-dried than they ever had before."

He turned to Brie. "Your mother tried to stop her, so Vera got rid of *her*, too. None of us in The Corporation knew what happened to her, and Vera refused to tell us. I found out only recently.

"The All-Seeing Eye's relationship to the Web was not just Read-Only. Vera also had the ability to edit sensitive documents and to create all-new ones. She sent your mother on a mission to Eastern Europe, and then, through some rewriting of documents, she made the Turkish government suspect that your mother was a spy. She was arrested and convicted."

"So she wasn't a criminal?" Brie asked.

"Your mother was the straightest of all straight arrows. But Vera was on a crusade. She had a messy world to tidy up, and she wouldn't let anybody get in her way. Not even her best friend."

He sighed. "Ever since then, Vera's been running the world. She issues mandates from her bunker here in the desert, and all of us Catalysts do what she says. Or at least we did—until recently."

He turned back to Brie. "When your mother was released from prison, things got pretty tense around here. Vera kept her under constant surveillance, worrying that she might try to come back to oppose her. Until tonight, your mother's been playing it safe: not using digital media, not going online at all—not even using a cell phone."

Brie remained quiet, but I could see her thinking.

"Tonight, Monica made her move. She called the Scenarios hotline and arranged a flight here. Vera knew it—and I'm sure your mother *knew* that she would know."

"And yet Vera allowed her to come," I said.

He nodded. "Right into her trap. So... this is what you've all blundered into. Tonight, the future of the Scenarios Division will be decided. A lot of us remember Monica, and a lot of others never knew her. We'll have a showdown, I'm pretty sure about that. But I can't be optimistic about the outcome."

He walked over to the soldier at the console. "Donovan's my right-hand man," he said. "I know I can trust him. I'm not sure about the rest of the guys under my command."

The soldier faced him. "You can trust them, sir. I keep telling you that."

"I hope you're right." He turned back to the rest of us. "But we all work for Vera. And I just can't be sure."

Our shuttle descended to a runway, and the helicopters landed all around us. As the soldiers climbed out of the choppers, they surrounded the shuttle. Donovan opened the shuttle door, and Gage escorted us out onto the tarmac. The air was warm, although it was now after midnight and the sky was still pitch black.

Monica's private jet was off to one side of the runway.

I turned to Gage. "Where is she now?"

"Unit 5 got to her before we did."

"And?"

"I don't know. But we're about to find out."

He and his soldiers led us toward a row of rectangular one-story shacks. They were sand-colored, and one entire side of each shack looked like a huge garage door. The door to one of the shacks opened as we approached. Inside was a vehicle resembling a single subway car, but it was turned the wrong way. Instead of its head facing outward, it was wedged sideways so snugly inside the shack that it couldn't possibly go anywhere. Or so I thought.

The doors of the subway car opened, and all of us boarded, including Gage's men.

"Pretty crowded in here," I said as the doors closed.

The soldiers were all holding onto a bar or a strap, but I couldn't understand why. As far as I could see, we were trapped.

"Better hang on to something," Gage warned us.

Just as we reached for the nearest bar or strap, the ground gave way beneath the subway car. We were in free-fall within some kind of elevator shaft, and through the windows we could see lights from the various floors flying past. We must've fallen twenty or thirty stories before the subway car began to decelerate, and another several stories before it slowed to a stop.

I took a deep breath and let go of the strap. "Everybody okay?"

"Better hang on," Gage told us. "We're not done yet."

Just as we reached out again, the subway car sped forward through a dark tunnel illuminated only by our headlights. It felt like we went from zero to one hundred in less than ten seconds. We raced through this tunnel for a few minutes until it looked like we were going to smash into a wall at the end of it. At the last minute, the subway car slowed to a stop.

The headlights turned off, leaving us in complete darkness. Gage's men stood at attention, readying their rifles.

Suddenly, one of the walls of the tunnel opened, and light poured in from a huge ballroom.

Gage whispered an expletive.

The place was filled with troops—all of them aiming their laser rifles at us.

Gage's men aimed back, ready to fire.

An old woman's voice came over a loudspeaker.

"Lieutenant Gage," she said. "Order your men to stand down."

He thought a moment, then nodded. "You heard her."

The soldiers around us lowered their weapons. The subway car's doors opened, and the troops outside motioned for us all to step out. One by one, Gage's men were disarmed.

As soon as we were all out of the subway car, the other soldiers surrounded us and herded us into the ballroom. They outnumbered The Cavalry three-to-one.

At the far side of the hall—the side they were pushing us toward—was a single high-backed swivel-chair facing away from us. The soldiers led us up to the chair and stopped.

Gage was on my left, with Woody, the Professor, Brie and L'Monjello on my right. The Cavalry was close behind us. The rest of the soldiers backed up and waited.

After a moment, the swivel chair turned, revealing a diminutive old lady in a colorless moo-moo. The right side of her head had white hair, uncombed. The left side was enclosed in an airtight glass case, rounded like a fishbowl. Her skull on that side had been removed down to her cheekbone, between her eye and her ear, putting her brain on display. A rectangular metal box was jammed tightly through her left eye socket, and a profusion of wires connected the metal box to the gray matter behind it.

As she turned to face us, her good eye moved around. But the metal box also had a prosthetic eye on the end of it, bulging out of her left socket. It didn't move, but just stared straight ahead.

"Now then," she said. "Let's get this party started!"

27 THE TRUTH, DAK

Vera rose from her seat and addressed the soldiers. As she stepped closer, I could see that she was wearing a headset microphone over her right ear.

"Darkness is covering the earth," she said, her rasping voice echoing through the hall. "The evil powers are trying to overcome the good. Whatever hope there may be for the world rests with us here. *Only* with us. If we survive, freedom will survive. But if we succumb to the forces of evil..."

She stopped mid-sentence and her one good eye whirled around and around. Her mouth made wild spasmodic movements, and she kept sticking out her tongue and pulling it back in again. She grunted and breathed irregularly into her microphone.

I leaned toward Gage. "What's happening?"

"She's answering a text message. She does it all in her head. She'll be done in a minute."

Just as he said that, the facial spasms stopped and she resumed her speech. "Tonight this sacred space has been invaded. This intrusion is more than just a personal insult. It's an assault on all that is good and just."

Again, her eye rolled around and her tongue stuck out.

I turned to Gage. "Does she do this often?"

He nodded. "She's always multi-tasking. You get used to it."

"The invasion has been stopped," she continued. "Tragedy has been averted. Once again, the All-Seeing Eye has saved the day."

Brie shook her head and whispered, "What a bunch of drivel!"

Vera turned, outraged. "Who dares interrupt the Supreme Commander?"

Nobody said anything.

Turning to our group, she looked us over one by one, then stopped in front of Brie. "You!"

Brie was unafraid. Turning to be heard by everyone in the hall, she announced, "I am the daughter of Monica DiMarco, and I'm here to see my mother!"

A mumbling sound swept the hall.

The old lady smiled unpleasantly. "Oh, how proud your mother must be of you. After all she's been through, what a great source of comfort it must be to her, to see what you've become."

Brie was flushed with anger. "After all *you* put her through, you mean."

"Yes, your mother must be very proud of you, parading around in your skimpy outfits and giggling with your little friends about nothing."

She turned back to the soldiers. "Have you heard what Monica DiMarco's daughter has done with her life? She's a TV star. She sings and dances and has fun all day on camera. She's been so busy living the life of a famous TV star that she's never had the slightest thought about her mother. And now she comes here... tonight of all nights... and plays for your sympathy. That's just a little too coincidental, don't you think?"

"I'm here because my mother is here," Brie said. "All my life, they told me she was dead. I learned the truth hours ago."

"You could've learned it years ago if you had wanted to. You've been too busy sprawling in front of the camera."

L'Monjello was mad. "Back off, lady! You have no clue what this girl's been through."

"Ah, young love," Vera said. "How sickening."

She turned to him and studied him a moment. "L'Monjello Parker. Star Student! Big deal!"

She took a few more steps and stopped in front of Woody. "You know why he went to The Valley, Mr. Wilson? Star Student that he is? Have you ever stopped to think why he's not at a brand-name institution?"

Woody looked nervous. "The Valley is a wonderful place. I'm sure he had his pick of schools!"

"He might've," she said, "if he had had the nerve to try."

She turned back to L'Monjello. "You never did. I know. I've got the All-Seeing Eye. You never applied anywhere except The Valley. What are you afraid of, L'Monjello Parker?"

"Nothing."

"Are you sure?"

"Positive."

"You just wanted to be a big fish in a little pond, eh? I think there's more to it. I think you're afraid to swim with the big fish."

He ground his teeth.

She turned back and put her face close to Brie's as if she were being confidential. "It's a personality trait with him," she whispered. "He does the same thing with women. Doesn't go out on dates. Just sits at home and watches you on TV. He thinks he loves you—you and only you—but how could that be? He's never met you until today. You know what I think? I think he's just been using you as an excuse to avoid real relationships. What do you think, Ms. DiMarco?"

"I think you need to get a life," said Brie.

"You should know all about that," Vera told her. "The wonderful life you lead. All on camera for the world to see."

"Leave her alone," L'Monjello said.

Vera mimicked a child's voice. "Yes, be nice to the poor girl. The poor little Valley Girl."

She stopped and stared into space.

A moment passed, and we all looked around at each other, wondering what was happening.

"Texting again?" I asked.

"No," Gage said, studying her face. "Her eyes aren't moving."

"Is she dead?"

"We can't be that lucky."

Then she moved her head a little and said, "Valley Girl." She took a few steps. "She's a Valley Girl." She paced and pondered what she had said. "Okay... fine." Staring off into space, she nodded. "For sure... For sure..."

"Oh, that," said Gage. "Lyrics get her every time."

She blinked. "Where was I?"

"You were going to take me to my mother," said Brie.

"Your mother doesn't work here anymore."

"We followed her here. And you know where she is."

"She shouldn't have come. She knows better."

"I demand that you take me to her."

"Or what? Is the widdle princess gonna have a tantwum? Grow up!"

I had had enough of this. "Look, lady. We came for Monica. Where is she?"

Vera walked over to me and sighed. "I've always liked you, Dak. But do you really want me to tell the others why you're here?"

My eyes narrowed. "What are you talking about?"

She chuckled and approached the Professor. "Aliens from outer space, Professor? Really?"

"Yes, madam!"

"Why don't you tell them the truth?"

He pondered his answer a moment. "I don't know what you mean," he stammered.

She paced back and forth in front of us a couple of times with her hands behind her back, waiting. Finally, she stopped and looked around at us. "There are no aliens from another planet," she announced. "The Professor has misled you."

I glanced at him, and then I stared. *He looked guilty!*

"Tell them the truth!" she said.

"I ha-ha-have told them!"

She smiled.

Woody broke the silence. "Professor... I trusted you against my better judgment. You have to tell us. What's she talking about?"

The Professor slumped over and shook his head. "I don't know."

The old lady paced again. "There is no creature from another galaxy on this earth. The Professor knows that I'm right."

He looked like he was going to cry.

L'Monjello addressed all of us. "Don't listen to her. She's trying to divide us."

"Big fish," she said. "Little pond." She walked back over to me and added, "Dak's known all along."

I refused to play into it.

"He's been working on his fallback position from Day One."

I saw the others looking at me, but I didn't return their gaze.

"He's writing a book. You're all in it. I've read his notes."

Woody took the bait. "Is that what you were doing earlier today?"

"Yes, Mr. Wilson, that's what he was doing. It's the most absurd little comedy. He makes you all look quite ridiculous."

"Dak? Is this true?"

It wasn't just Woody. Everybody wanted to know.

My throat was dry. "Look, lady, I see how you are, and I'm not falling for it."

I turned to the others. "L'Monjello's right. Everything she says is true... up to a point. There's enough factual content in it to incriminate every one of us. She's putting the wrong slant on it. What she's saying is true, and yet it's a lie. Don't you get it?"

Nobody looked very happy with me, except the old lady. "You're a smart one, Dak. You've always been my favorite minion."

I whirled on her. "I don't work for you!"

"The truth, Dak. You said it yourself. I'm telling the truth. You've done my bidding for years, quite willingly; and I've rewarded you well.

Whatever fame you have is due to me."
 "I don't know what you're talking about."
 "Allow me to introduce myself," she said. "I'm Deep Throat!"

28 SHOWDOWN

I felt the world collapse beneath my feet. I stared into her hideous face and saw my whole life in a new light. All these years, I had been nothing but a puppet—*her* puppet!

She cackled. "The truth hurts—eh, Dak?"

Returning to Brie, she said, "Your mother was a spy. She was given a fair trial and found guilty."

"You are a dictator and a murderer," Brie said. "My mother tried to stop you, so you framed her. Everyone in this room knows it's true. If anyone here has a shred of integrity left, now is the time to show it!"

Vera was furious. "Look who's talking: the TV bimbo. What do you know about integrity?"

L'Monjello stepped toward her, but Brie stopped him.

Then another woman's voice came over the loudspeaker: "Don't believe everything you see on TV, Vera."

The old lady was outraged. Her good eye twirled around and around, and she stuck her tongue in and out furiously. At her bidding, a trap door opened in the floor and an old-fashioned pillory rose into view. Monica's head and hands stuck out of it.

Soldiers throughout the hall cried out in disapproval, but Vera was too busy to notice. She rushed over to the pillory and pulled a headset microphone off Monica's ear.

"How did you get this?" she demanded.

Monica smirked. "We spies are a sneaky lot."

"Mom!" Brie shouted.

"I'm all right, Cambria. Stay where you are."

Gage and his men hurried over and formed a ring around her, protecting her from the rest of Vera's army.

One of them turned to Gage. "Told you, sir."

"You were right, Donovan, I should've listened to you."

He spoke to the old lady. "It's over, Vera. Set Monica free."

"Gage, you disappoint me," she told him. "I always knew you were a traitor, but I thought you were smarter than this. You have no weapons. You can't get out of here alive. You and your men are making the ultimate sacrifice—for nothing."

As she spoke, soldiers all around the room broke rank and joined Gage's men.

Vera was surprised, but not alarmed. "It doesn't matter. You're still outnumbered. You'll never get out alive."

"Don't be so sure about that."

He pressed a button on his belt and the lights went out. Pandemonium followed as Vera's men ran forward to do battle with the soldiers on Gage's side. I grabbed the Professor and hit the ground. Woody followed my lead.

I could hear Gage's voice above the din. "That was me, Donovan."

"Sorry, sir."

"Good punch, though. Keep it up."

"Yes, sir."

Using a flashlight, L'Monjello and Brie hurried to Monica and released her from the pillory. Mother and daughter enjoyed a brief embrace.

Then Monica said, "We've got to find Vera. If she doesn't cooperate with the Professor, the whole world's done for."

L'Monjello moved the flashlight around until it reflected off the glass cover of the All-Seeing Eye. Vera was weaving her way through the crowd, trying to reach the subway car.

Monica raced across the room and knocked her to the ground.

"Whoa!" said L'Monjello. "That glass in Vera's head must be shatter-proof. Did you see how she landed?"

Brie started after them, but he stopped her.

"Better let your mom handle this one. She's been looking forward to this for fifteen years."

The soldiers continued fighting in the dark as the rest of us stayed low.

"Gage's men are still outnumbered," Woody said. "What can we do to help?"

"Noble thought, Woody, but I'm willing to bet you're no good in a fight. And the Professor here..."

Suddenly, at the far side of the room, the wall opened up beside the subway car and bright lights shined in on us. A new car had arrived, filled with journalists. Fru Phillips was one of them, shouting commentary as he ran into the action.

"No!" I shouted. "The Press! Naif warned me about this."

"Yes I did, but you wouldn't listen."

I looked up, and there was Naif, standing above me, taping the whole thing with a night scope. "The other networks are messing it up with those bright lights. It was a good show before that."

"How long have you been here?"

"Long enough to learn you're writing a book. I hope I'm in it."

"You were here even then?"

"Before that, actually. I posed as one of the soldiers. None of them noticed, but the other networks followed me. And Roi DiMarco's goons, of course."

"They're here, too?"

Just then, another subway car pulled up, and gangsters came in shooting ray guns. Soldiers all over the room shot back with *their* ray guns and a battle ensued.

"Naif, get down!" I said.

Bodies fell everywhere—a few here, a dozen there.

"Naif!"

He was moving forward to see better when one of the rays hit him and he collapsed several feet away from me.

Meanwhile, shadowy figures emerged from all corners of the room, leaping and dancing around the blasts from the ray guns. Some of them had what looked like catcher's mitts, which they used to trap the deadly rays. Others shot back with devices that jammed the rays at their source.

Gangsters and soldiers alike showed exasperation as they tried to shoot but couldn't.

To add to the confusion, a barroom piano began to play. Everybody stopped in amazement.

A spotlight was aimed on the pianist. It was one of the Clayborn Clones, dressed in a tuxedo and top hat. Then the spotlight widened to reveal another clone dressed the same way, lying on top of the piano. The second one began singing:

> *There's something new*
> *Under the sun...*

Their siblings burst in from all directions, dancing to Big Band accompaniment:

> *We are The One That Is Many,*

Ronald R. Johnson

The Many That Are One!

Some of Vera's soldiers lunged forward and tried to pounce on them. Grabbing the soldiers' hands, they forced them to join the dance. Then they surrounded them with ropes and pulled them together into bundles. The good soldiers went around collecting them.

They thought we were finished,
But we've just begun.
We are The One That Is Many,
The Many That Are One!

Now they took out huge clubs and used them on the thugs and the rest of Vera's soldiers. Sumo Carl, also in a tux, seemed to enjoy the work. Soldiers flew in every direction. Gage's men gathered them up where they landed.

If you're plotting evil,
You'd better run.
'Cuz we're The One That Is Many,
The Many That Are One!

A clone stepped forward to do a trumpet riff as two others escorted Vera to the pillory and locked her in.

Don't know what the future holds
But it's sure to be fun.
For we're The One That Is Many,
The Many That are One!

The drums signaled a big finish as the boys formed a chorus line with Sumo Carl in the center.

We are The One That Is Many!
(Bump-bump TEE bump)
Yes, we're The One That Is Many!
(Bumpity bumpity bumpity)
We're The One That Is Many!
(Bump! Bump!)
The Many That Are One!

Fru Phillips was shouting over the music: "Ladies and gentlemen,

I've never seen anything like it! Part crime-fighting, part cabaret! Pleasing... yet strangely disturbing!"

When the lights came back on, I hurried over to Naif. He had died instantly.

"Poor guy!" Woody said. "He took one right through the lens."

I struggled to speak. "Just the way he would've wanted it."

Gage and his soldiers gathered up DiMarco's goons and Vera's men and herded them onto subway cars. After they were gone, the soldiers turned to the journalists.

Fru Phillips whined. "What about Dak? Why does he get to stay?"

But Gage wasn't listening. He had a logistical problem, and he called to the clones. "Hey! Do you guys want to help?"

Within a minute or two, the clones had rounded up all the journalists (except me, of course) and put them on the last of the subway cars.

"Make sure they find their way out," Gage told the clones. And they sped out of sight.

One of his men, returning from a side room, handed Gage the Communicator. Holding it carefully in both hands, Gage approached Monica with a martial step and stood at attention before her.

"It's good to have you back, Commander," he said. "Will you do us the honor?"

She took the Communicator from his hands. "Thank you, Lieutenant. Please convey to your men my deep appreciation for their service."

He nodded and backed away.

Monica turned to the Professor. "Come with me."

Together, they went to Vera, who was locked in the pillory. Brie and L'Monjello, Woody, and I gathered around them.

The look that the two women exchanged was not what I expected. There was no hatred, nor did Vera show any sign of resistance. Monica reached out with the device, and Vera took it willingly in one of her immobilized hands.

As soon as she touched it, the Communicator displayed an image the Professor knew all too well. He was so stunned, he nearly fell backwards.

"Basil!" he said.

29 GOING BERSERK

The Professor stared at Vera in disbelief.

She dropped the Communicator at her feet and laughed hysterically. "Oh, Professor! How surprised you look!"

"You know him! You lied to us!"

"I told you the truth," she said. "You refuse to believe it."

"You must take us to him."

"I will not. You were all just pawns. It's me he wants. I've got the All-Seeing Eye. But he'll never have me."

"You must lead us to him! We'll all be destroyed if you don't."

"Yes, yes, I know about that" she said. "Good riddance, I say. We'll all be better off."

He started to object, but she interrupted him. "Oh come now, Professor! You know what it's like. You wanted to get away from the human race, too. You fled to the moon to leave us all behind." She sighed. "Oh, how I envied you! I can't even close my eyes in sleep. The whole world's here with me. Right here!" She tried to point toward the metal box in her eye. "Day and night! Never a moment's rest. But I will rest soon. That's all I live for now. The world will end... and then... I can rest." She closed her one good eye, smiling.

While all this was going on, Monica turned to Brie and touched her face lovingly. Brie responded by placing her own hand on top of her mother's and gazing back at her with deep concern. Turning to L'Monjello, Monica gave him that same look she had given him back at her apartment. He nodded, but he, too, appeared worried. As she turned away, both of them reached out to stop her, unsuccessfully.

Vera's good eye was still closed. Monica approached the pillory and called her name, startling her.

"We're going to see Basil now," Monica told her. "Together."

Vera stared at her in horror. "I can't!" she said. "I can't!"

"You can, and you will."

"No! No!" She looked panicked. "You don't know what he's like!"

"You're right. I don't know anything about him. But you've got to go to him. I'll be right there with you."

"You must to listen to me! I can't go! How can I make you understand?"

She was fighting so hard to free herself that the pillory bounced in place. The Communicator rolled underneath her.

"I can't! I can't!"

I turned to the Professor, who had backed away in revulsion.

"She looks terrified!" I said.

He nodded, and he seemed rattled himself.

"What do you know about Basil?" I asked.

He shook his head.

Vera had worked herself into such hysterics that Monica couldn't reason with her.

"I won't go! I won't go! I won't go! I won't go!"

Her wrists and neck bled as she tried to break free.

"I won't go! I won't go!"

And while she repeated this mantra, her one good eye whirled around and around.

Suddenly, an alarm went off.

"This place is about to blow," Gage said.

There were no subway cars left.

He signaled The Cavalry and they sprang into action. Within seconds, they donned jetpacks and hurried toward us.

One of them grabbed me from behind and lifted me off my feet. Others helped Woody and the Professor. L'Monjello and Brie tried to resist.

"Mom!" Brie shouted.

We all raced upward toward open air ducts in the ceiling. The next thing we knew, we were flying through dark shafts that zigzagged left then right, vertical then horizontal. There was more than one path upward, and from time to time the Cavalrymen would separate into thinner tunnels, then re-emerge and fly as a group, only to split up again. We were going so fast, we almost hit the walls of the shaft as we rounded each corner.

A computerized voice began a countdown. I couldn't hear the numbers over the noise of the jetpacks, but I sensed that we accelerated even more once the countdown started. Then the voice stopped, and from far down the shaft, I could hear a deep percussive roar like an earthquake. It grew louder and louder, and the walls of the shaft began to shake.

The soldier carrying me said, "Hang on!"

I closed my eyes as the walls crumbled around us.

"Almost there!" he said.

When I opened my eyes, we were all out in the night air, flying higher and higher into the sky as the ground below us burst into flames. The whole canyon gave way to one explosion after another. We could feel the heat. Our guides lifted us far above it all, and finally found a cliff where we could safely land.

Brie and L'Monjello ran from one rescuer to the next, pleading.

"What about my mother?"

"Did Monica make it?"

Finally they found Gage. He had stayed longer than the others, and his fatigues were smoldering.

He shook his head. "I tried to get her to come with me," he told them, "but she wouldn't leave. She said Vera was our only hope." Turning to Brie, he added, "She told me to make sure you were safe."

Brie just stared at him.

"Your mother was the bravest person I ever knew," he said. "You should be very proud of her, ma'am."

She turned to L'Monjello, then back to Gage.

"I..."

She stopped, shook her head, and tried again.

"I'm not sure what to think. I wish I could've known her."

He nodded. "I'm sorry for your loss, ma'am."

He and the Cavalry regrouped and talked about what to do next. A moment later, they flew us across the canyon and back to our shuttle. The journalists and the clones were there waiting for us.

"Dak!" Fru shouted. "Tell us what's happening!"

I ignored him. I knew we had bigger problems.

The Professor took me aside and whispered: "The Communicator..."

"Yes, I know," I told him. "It rolled under the pillory, last I saw."

He gave me a hard look. "Do you remember what the aliens said would happen?"

I nodded.

Just then, we heard a noise above our heads. It sounded like a welding machine, only louder. We looked up and saw a bright light—like a huge star in the black sky. It sputtered and crackled, and from out of it a bolt of lightning ripped across the heavens and stopped at another point. Now there were two bright star-like objects, both sputtering and crackling, with a line of light connecting them, slightly arched. From those two points, other arcs of light shot out in all directions across the sky, louder and louder until the night was ablaze with sizzling dots connected by lines of lightning.

Brie reached out to L'Monjello.

Woody approached us. "What is it, Doc?"

The Professor's face was gaunt. "It's the end of the world, Mr. Wilson."

30 THE NET OF FIRE

Within minutes, the entire planet was surrounded by the strange network of light. Websites and news outlets all around the world reported the same thing we were seeing.

Each nation sent its Air Force up to investigate, but no one was able to pass through the net of fire. Some shot missiles at it, to no avail.

"What does it mean?" I asked the Professor. "Is it going to close in on us?"

L'Monjello had been working on that very question. After taking pictures of the net of fire and doing an online image search, he discussed his findings with the clones. After much deliberation, they made up their minds.

Leading the group over to the Professor and me, L'Monjello spoke. "We think we know what this is."

After we were seated back inside the shuttle, L'Monjello explained. "We're unable to tell what kind of substance it is. It seems more like electricity than fire, but we don't know how the aliens are generating it or what's sustaining it. We'll let the scientists figure that out. But we think we know what it's for.

"We believe it's a clue," he said. "Since we don't have the Communicator anymore, the aliens are advising us on how to proceed."

One of the clones spoke up. "There's a pattern to this network. The dots are connected by curved lines. Some have many lines emanating from them while others have only a few."

L'Monjello showed us his cell phone. "I found a diagram from the

1960s that has an almost identical pattern. It's from a study done by the social psychologist Stanley Milgram. He called it 'The Small World Experiment.' Milgram wanted to know why complete strangers so often discover that they're connected in some way—that they have a mutual friend or acquaintance. So he set up an experiment to learn about the various links between two people on opposite ends of the continent: Person A and Person B. His study showed that any two people, chosen randomly, are connected in some way by a network of friends, and that, on average, it takes only five or six links to get from one to the other."

"I've heard of that," Woody said. "It's called 'Degrees of Separation,' isn't it?"

"That's the popular version of it," L'Monjello told him. "But it's based on Milgram's research."

One of the clones explained. "Each dot represents a person. Some people know lots of others, so there are many lines coming out of them. Others know only a few."

"Like us," said another clone. "We only know each other."

"Or me," said Brie. "I only know people from the show."

"But when we all work together," L'Monjello said, "it's possible for any individual anywhere to be introduced to any other individual, no matter who they are. We've all just got to rely on our network of acquaintances to help us get there."

The Professor was fascinated. "So what do you believe the aliens are trying to tell us?"

"We don't need the Communicator to lead us to Basil," L'Monjello replied. "Every person in the world is connected to him in some way, through the people they already know. We've all just got to tap into our social networks."

"What's your recommendation?" I asked.

"Get on your phones," he said. "Contact everyone you know. Tell them we need their help finding Basil. Ask *them* to contact everyone *they* know. And so on. And ask them to report back to you as soon as they hear something."

I turned to the Professor. "What do you think?"

He nodded. "I think Mr. Parker and his friends are right. But there's one more thing."

He looked around at all of us. "If our own experience of the past few days is any indication, we should pay special heed to the people we would most wish *not* to talk to—those who are different from us, those whom we find it difficult to understand. If there are people whose ideas or habits are incompatible with ours, those are the ones we should especially seek out.

"Don't just ask for their help finding Basil. Take time to talk to them. It may be the last chance you'll ever have. And if we survive this crisis, tell them that you'll keep them in your heart, come what may. No matter how deeply you disagree with their ideas or the direction they're going in life, tell them you will always try to think well of them and wish the best for them. And mean it."

We were silent for a long, awkward moment. Even *I* didn't dare to say what I was thinking.

Finally L'Monjello spoke for all of us. "I wonder how many people can keep a promise like that?"

The Professor shook his head. "Not many, I would guess. Some will resolve to do it and give up. But a few here or there may actually see it through... and perhaps those few will be enough to save us all."

So we got on our phones, and what happened over the next several hours was unprecedented in the history of the world. It started with our little group, but the numbers grew exponentially and soon surrounded the globe.

Woody reached out to his fan base, and they, in turn, reached outward by the hundreds, then thousands, then tens of thousands.

L'Monjello talked to faculty and staff at The Valley. Within minutes, everyone on campus knew, and they relied on their personal and professional networks to get the word out to universities and communities all over the world.

I walked over to the Press Pool with the Professor and we explained what was happening. Fru was there, but I ignored him. When they ran off to make their reports, I called the office and talked to Maggie and Dodge. We mourned the loss of Naif, but we couldn't let that slow us down. I called everybody I'd ever interviewed, every professional contact, every friend or foe.

I heard the Professor talking to his old Ivy League cronies, but he called lots of other people, too. I was surprised when he called the folks back home. He was from the Ozarks, although I never would've guessed that. And many of them, it turns out, were good sources of information.

Brie called her Uncle Roi. "We can argue about that later," she told him. "Right now we've got to work together." They arranged a satellite hook-up, and before long, she was talking to her TV audience of middle schoolers, asking them not to be afraid. "I'm looking for the person who can stop all this," she told them. "And I need your help."

It will go down in the history books as Small World Day.

For that one day, the whole human race connected. We listened to each other. We cared. We pronounced blessings upon people we ordinarily would have cursed. And most importantly, we cooperated with each other. Everybody everywhere dropped what they were doing and joined in a common pursuit: to find this one alien person whose whereabouts meant life or death for us all.

Although the clones only knew each other and the few people they had met on earth over the past few days, they didn't remain idle. They were doing something online, and they seemed quite intent on it. As the day progressed, I kept hearing them repeat the word "kindred." I thought it was strange the first time they said it. It was an old-fashioned word, and "kindred" was the one thing they didn't have. But they said it over and over, and they became quite agitated about it.

At first I thought they were having an argument, but then I realized they were problem-solving. Tension seemed to grow as they discussed this "kindred" issue, but then they formed some sort of consensus. They lined up and did that unique handshake they had done on the moon: each one grabbing one brother's arm with his left hand and another brother's arm with his right.

"The One That Is Many," one would say, and the other would reply, "The Many That Are One."

They looked grim but proud. There was a special light in their eyes.

Then they climbed into their individual space pods and flew away, each in a different direction.

My phone rang and Woody's face appeared.

He was beaming. "Dak! We found him. We found Basil!"

31 RENDEZVOUS

I looked around and was surprised that Woody, L'Monjello, and Brie were all missing. Acting on a tip, they had gotten a ride with a television crew to check it out. In all the confusion, I hadn't even seen them go. I called the Professor over, then returned to Woody.

"Where are you?" I asked.

"You'll never believe it: the YMCA of the Rockies! In Estes Park!"

I turned to the Professor. "While we're scouring the earth to locate him, he's relaxing at a resort."

"Not exactly," said Woody. "This is just where he ended up earlier today, after the rescue."

"What rescue?"

"A mentally-handicapped man lost in the mountains. Search parties had given up on him, especially when the net of fire appeared. Then the two of them turned up in the park this morning. Basil had found him and brought him back."

He panned the scene with his phone. "Lots of people are here now: not only the search parties and the media, but many others. Everybody in the world is looking for him, of course, and word's gotten out that he's here. Quite a crowd's gathering. Better hurry if you want to meet him."

"We're on our way," I said.

But as the Professor and I rode the shuttle north to Colorado, I couldn't conceal my anger. Of course I was mad that members of "the media" were there ahead of me, but my real complaint was hanging over our heads. "We found him. So why is the net of fire still in the sky?"

"He's waiting for us," the Professor replied.

"You mean *you*."

"No. Both of us."

"What does he want from me?"

He shook his head.

As we got closer, Woody called us again. "Are you guys coming?"

"We'll be there soon," I told him. "Have you met him?"

"Oh, yes! Everybody here has. He's quite gregarious. Turns out he's made lots of friends in the past week but nobody knew who he was."

I frowned. "What's your take on him? What's he want from us?"

Woody grinned. "You know…" He shrugged and searched for a way to explain. "He doesn't seem to want anything personally." He scratched the back of his neck and grinned again. "And yet… everybody comes away with work to do. Brie's a prime example. She cried and cried when she talked to him."

"Really? She doesn't seem like the weepy type."

"That's what *she* kept saying. But she figured her life out while talking to Basil. It's starting to make sense to her, at least. She knows what she has to do now."

"What is he, some kind of self-help guru?"

Woody started to laugh, then stopped and reconsidered. He was about to answer again but paused and shook his head. "I'd better let you decide for yourself."

It wasn't long before the shuttle descended toward our destination. As we hovered over the park, we could see people everywhere.

"It's like a rock concert down there," I said.

L'Monjello, Brie, and Woody waited for our shuttle to land, then Woody rushed forward as we stepped out.

"Man, am I glad you two made it! We think he's getting ready to leave."

We worked our way through the crowd.

"Dak!" a voice called.

It was Fru Phillips. He had followed us there and was running to catch up.

"Ignore him," I told the others, and we kept walking. They escorted us to a heavy-set middle-aged man. Beside him was a big dog.

"Basil!" I said. "Why is the net of fire still in the sky? We've found you! The game's over!"

The man laughed, "Ha-ha! Yeah!"

"Don't you understand?" I asked. "We did our part; now you do yours. Get rid of the net of fire."

He laughed again and nodded. "Basil good boy!"

"What are you talking about? You're not good at all! You're threatening to destroy the world."

"Basil *very* good boy!"

I turned to Woody and scowled. "This man is an idiot!"

Woody and the others were laughing so hard, they were doubled over. The Professor grabbed my arm. "Not him! *Him!*"

I glanced over and found the dog looking back at me. I couldn't tell what breed he was, but he was a magnificent looking creature. There was intelligence in his face, and around his neck was a collar with a miniature Communicator.

The Professor knelt down and touched the device. "It's in English!"

"Of course it is," said Woody. "How do you think he's been talking to the rest of us?"

I was annoyed. "Then why didn't he speak English all along?"

No one bothered to answer me. The Professor was reading the message on the monitor. "It's for me!" he said.

Then he read it aloud, barely above a whisper:

> *I fled Him, down the nights and down the days;*
> *I fled Him, down the arches of the years;*
> *I fled Him, down the labyrinthine ways*
> *Of my own mind; and in the mist of tears*
> *I hid from Him, and under running laughter.*

The Professor's eyes narrowed and he thought very hard about this cryptic passage. Then he gazed into the dog's face in amazement, as if he suddenly recognized him.

Another message appeared on the screen:

> *Across the margent of the world I fled,*
> *And troubled the gold gateways of the stars,*
> *Smiting for shelter on their clanged bars;*
> *Fretted to dulcet jars*
> *And silvern chatter the pale ports o' the moon.*

The moon!

The Professor stared at the Communicator and said nothing for a long time. Then, almost shyly, he raised his eyes to meet Basil's. He asked quietly:

> *Is my gloom, after all,*
> *Shade of Thine hand, outstretched caressingly?*

They looked deeply into one another's eyes. At first the Professor seemed awed, but then his brow furrowed as if he were thinking something over. After a while he nodded and grinned, and his grin slowly broadened into a jubilant smile. He rose and somehow seemed taller than before, his shoulders squarer, head higher.

"Please come closer," he urged everyone. "Basil has asked me to speak on his behalf."

32 WE ARE NOT ALONE

The crowd huddled around the Professor. Someone stuck a microphone in his hand.

"For over a century," he said, "we have explored the heavens in search of intelligent life. 'We are not alone,' we have told ourselves. We have sent out our probes and have waited for a message from Beyond. Now that message has come. You and I have been summoned to this place to hear it. And the message is: we are *not* alone."

A shiver of excitement rushed through the crowd at these words. But the Professor looked around at us sternly and continued.

"Earth holds more ants than humans. The cockroach was here thousands of years before we were. This planet is teeming with alien societies. Search the grass, the trees, the sky, the oceans. We are not alone."

People glanced at each other uncomprehendingly.

He continued. "When will we take seriously the lives of people in other cultures? 'How exotic!' we say as we step foot on their shores. Then we buy their souvenirs and dismiss the people and their struggles from our minds. Alien life on other planets? There is alien life all over *this* planet. We have not tuned our ears to hear what other cultures are saying to us. Listen. *We are not alone!*"

Many in the crowd fidgeted, but some nodded.

"We think we know our neighbors because we can name the party they vote for or the music they listen to. We think we know our colleagues because we've read their résumés. Our cameras have entered one another's living rooms and dining rooms and bedrooms... and we conclude that there's nothing left to learn about each other.

"But what do we know of the inner lives of those around us? What do

120

we know about the stirrings in their souls? How can we say who they're capable of becoming?

"'We are not alone,' we say, and we look to the stars. We should lower our eyes and look at one another. The person beside us is more alien than we realize.

"We are not alone!"

All around me I could see people catching on, then trying to explain it to those beside them. The Professor continued, undaunted.

"We say we care about the needy because we give to our favorite charity. But why do we allow poverty and injustice to continue at all? We say that our government exists for us and that our elected officials are our public servants. Then why do we not raise a mighty cry against injustice? Why do we let it continue? Because it does not directly affect *us?* Open your hearts! Hear the cries of people in need! *We are not alone!"*

When he said these last words, many people nodded and mouthed them in unison. I looked around, bewildered. The Professor seemed to be getting the crowd on his side. His grizzled mane flowed behind him in the breeze, giving him the look of a modern-day prophet. I had never seen him like this before.

I was obviously missing something. Was there anyone else like me? I searched the crowd for signs and stopped at a sympathetic face. It was Basil's. He was gazing directly at me. I was about to look away when something happened. I guess it was telepathy. Somehow we had a conversation. He said he knew I would've preferred to play the role of a journalist right now, but he reminded me I could still write about this in my book.

"You know about that?" I asked.

Yes, he knew. The book would bring the gift of laughter to many people, he said. But the message was the important thing.

"What message!" I snorted. "I don't understand any of this!"

His eyes smiled. "That's why I chose you."

Now the refrain was thunderous: *"We are not alone!"*

"All the previous aeons have come down to this moment," the Professor continued. "All the lives that have ever been lived have come down to our lives now. Everyone who has ever hoped or feared or toiled on this earth is part of the fabric of our being. Their struggles have paved the way for ours, as ours will for those after us. We have inherited their ideas, their institutions, and their problems. They are with us whether we recognize their presence or not."

The crowd roared again: *"We are not alone!"*

"This is the great secret we humans were meant to learn. This is the one fact we ignore at our peril. There is far, far more to being human than any of us can become on our own. We are all in this together. Our only hope of becoming a truly human race is for each of us to commit ourselves to this principle and let it guide everything we do."

"We—are—not—alone!"

Suddenly there was a disturbance as a dozen men in uniform marched through the thick of the crowd, two abreast, and worked their way toward the Professor. It was The Cavalry, and Gage led the way. When they reached the front, the phalanx opened and a human figure slowly stepped out, leaning heavily on a cane.

Brie gasped. Rushing forward, she threw herself into her mother's arms, almost knocking her off her feet. L'Monjello followed close behind. Smiling at him, Monica stroked her daughter's hair gently, and the words that fell from her lips sounded like a song.

"My beautiful Cambria," she said.

Woody, who was standing beside me, laid his head on my shoulder and cried noisily. I held up my necktie. "Why don't you blow your nose while you're at it? Hey—I was joking!"

The mentally-challenged man raised his voice. "Basil! Basil? Here, boy! Now where that dog go?"

Everybody looked around. Where *had* he gone?

Throughout the crowd, people started pointing toward the sky. The net of fire had been replaced by a light so bright, we could hardly look upon it.

Then something happened that I don't know how to describe. It appeared as if the heavens were opened. For a moment we could see the inner workings of the universe—the real source of power behind this world we take for granted. All around me, people dropped to their knees. Others fell backwards. I grabbed a nearby post to steady myself.

Then it was gone.

There was absolute silence as the crowd gazed heavenward as if in a trance. I could hardly breathe, but with great difficulty I stumbled over to the Professor.

"Pr...Pr..."

I couldn't even say his name.

Gulping, I stared at the sky a moment, shook my head, and started over. "My... *God*... Professor!"

His face was radiant.

"Indeed!" he said.

33 THE REST OF THE STORY

For the next seven days I was busier than I had ever been before. With my new cameraman, Johnny Dominguez, I worked around the clock to keep up with the breaking news. The other networks did, too, and for the first time in our lives, we all shared information. This story was too big for any of us. We had to work together to get it right.

I'm not just talking about the net of fire and the strange events surrounding its appearance—and disappearance. I'm talking about the story behind the story.

On Small World Day, while people everywhere were reconnecting and sharing long-held secrets, rumors spread about an undercover organization called The Kindred. They had an enormous membership, from every nation on the globe. Authorities had been alarmed about them for some time, but it was impossible to get intelligence. On Small World Day, people came forward with what they knew, and it was as bad as authorities had feared. The organization had achieved victories in all the major governments, placing operatives in command of nuclear arsenals. But still, they couldn't take action because they didn't know who was part of the conspiracy and who wasn't.

Then came the final puzzle pieces: a team of young men fanned out all over the globe, giving authorities inside information. All these men looked and talked the same. Their fingerprints and DNA matched those of Carl Clayborn, one of The Kindred's early founders. These were the clones that Clayborn had taken up to the moon with him years ago. He had been grooming them to come back someday and assume command of the organization. Instead, they gave law enforcement officials the names and contact information of its key players. Best of all, they offered their services. Impersonating Clayborn, they infiltrated secret hideouts and led authorities to the conspirators.

Not all of these young men survived.

But their sacrifice was not in vain. The Kindred was shut down overnight. And that's when the startling truth was revealed. The organization had become apocalyptic in its final days. They no longer believed they could rule the world. Their latest plan was to destroy it.

They had set the date for the 24th.

As the news came out bit by bit, people all over the world wanted to meet the young men who had risked their lives to save us, but they disappeared as quickly as they had come. They told the authorities that they might resurface anywhere... anytime... whenever they were truly needed.

When asked for their names, each young man gave the same answer:

The One That Is Many
The Many That Are One

I was back in the office for the first time in two weeks. It was a strange feeling. Naif was alive the last time I was here. A lot had changed.

Dodge greeted me warmly. He wasn't mad at me anymore, even though I had run off to the moon without telling him and hadn't been back since. All's well that ends well.

Maggie, my personal assistant, was also conciliatory. She had been quite upset with me for not checking in, but Small World Day changed all that. Still...

"Now that you're here," she said, "would you please—*please*—get Fru Phillips off my back?"

"What does he want?"

"He left you a message this morning."

We went to my cubicle and I brought the video up on my computer.

"Hey, Dak. Fru here. I, uh... I don't know how to say this, so I'll just come out with it. Well... first... I'm sorry about Naif. He was a great guy, and I know that was quite a blow. I mean that. But the reason for my call is... well... I've never believed in... you know... religion... but on Small World Day, something happened... and I think you know what it was. I can't stop obsessing about it. This isn't professional... it's personal. I want to—" He shook his head. "I *need* to know. I'd like to talk to you about it. Please. No cameras, no recording equipment. Just man to man."

With a press of a button, I deleted the message.

Maggie was shocked. "That's it? Just delete it and forget about it?"

"That's right."

"*You* don't have to deal with him. I do."

"Maggie..."

"I'm not letting this go." And she stomped out of my cubicle.

I had a few loose ends to tie up, so I started at the top of my list.

I dialed Woody's number and his wife Edna appeared on the screen.

"Dak!" she said. "We've been glued to our sets for days. I mean, the world was almost destroyed! We can't believe it."

"Me neither," I said. "But you know what's even more unbelievable? Woody Wilson was a key player in it all! Who would've thought!"

She beamed. "Would you like to talk to him? He's on the other computer Skyping L'Monjello. Hang on and I'll tell him."

The screen went black, then it was split three ways: Brie and Monica were sitting together in the left panel, L'Monjello was in the middle, and Woody was on the right. It was total bedlam as we all shouted hellos to each other at once.

Monica had cleaned up well, both literally and figuratively. For the first time, I could see the resemblance between mother and daughter. She had a cast on her leg.

After the initial greetings, I asked her, "How did you survive the explosion?"

She smiled and nodded. "It was quite amazing, wasn't it?"

"Yes it was," I said. "But you didn't answer my question."

"Oh." Then she just looked at me.

L'Monjello and Brie caught each other's eye and smirked.

I waited another moment. "Okay. Let me rephrase the question. If *you* made it out alive, then what about Vera?"

"What *about* Vera?"

Brie and L'Monjello could no longer contain their laughter, and Woody applauded.

"Bravo!" he said.

Meanwhile, Monica and I were staring each other down. I waited a moment, but her eyes told me all I needed to know. She wasn't going to budge.

"You win, Monica. I give up."

"She's good," said Woody.

"You have no idea," L'Monjello told him.

"This isn't a question," I said, "just an observation. You and Brie seem pretty comfortable with each other."

They both smiled. "We've got a lot of catching up to do," Monica said.

"And we're running out of time," Brie added. "She'll be going back to work soon."

Monica looked at her.

"Oops," said Brie. "I'm not good at keeping secrets."

Monica turned back to me and grew serious. "I don't mean to be disrespectful to your line of work, Dak, but what I do requires utmost secrecy. For a brief time, all of you were allowed a glimpse of it. That cannot continue. I hope you understand that."

I thought she was talking to me, but all of us nodded solemnly and said Yes in unison.

She turned to Brie. "I just hope you can believe that my intentions are honorable... and always have been."

Brie was serious now, too. "I know, Mom," she said. "I know."

Monica excused herself at that point, and as she left the screen, Brie told us they were going shopping later this morning. "I've decided to redo my wardrobe... to match the new Me."

L'Monjello chimed in. "She's going back on the air. But on her own terms."

"I'm taking over the show," she explained. "I met with Uncle Roi and made sure he understood the gravity of his situation. He could spend the next several years in prison, or he could walk away. He made a wise decision. It helped that Mom was with me."

L'Monjello added, "Monica can be quite persuasive."

"She let me do the talking," said Brie. "But her presence had the desired effect."

I grinned. "I'm sure your uncle was thrilled to see his sister again after all these years."

"So thrilled he could hardly speak," she said. "He was even more excited when I reminded him about the money he owes me. But I was reasonable. I gave him a timetable for repayment. Meanwhile, he's turning the show over to me. I've spoken with my sponsors, and many of them are still on board."

"She's got some exciting plans," said L'Monjello.

"I'm going to be a real student!" she said. "And the show will focus on the things I'm learning. I just keep remembering what the Professor said that night in the park... about how little we know of the life around us. There's so much I want to learn! I'll broadcast the show for an hour or two, a few times a week, sharing the things I'm taking away from my classes."

Woody was elated. "What an inspiration you'll be to all those kids

126

who follow you online!"

"I hope so, Woody. If I can turn some of them on to learning, then maybe the show will be worth something after all."

"That's the other part of it," L'Monjello told us. "She's going to make the program more interactive."

She nodded. "I just keep wondering: Who *are* these kids? What are their interests? I want to learn more about them and see how I can help them."

"Are you going to take classes at The Valley?" I asked.

"For now," she said.

"But I offered her an alternative for the future," said L'Monjello.

She smiled back at him. "Our Star Student has been accepted to graduate school at the University of Chicago," she told us. "And he and I have become kind of inseparable..."

"...so I asked her to come with me..."

"...and I told him I would on one condition..."

"...which was really what I wanted anyway, but thought it might be too soon to ask her..."

Then they both said: "We're engaged!"

"We haven't set a date yet," he said.

"But I want to join him in Chicago as soon as possible," she said.

Woody and I shouted over each other congratulating them.

Once the commotion died down, I turned to Woody. "What are *your* plans?"

"Nothing that exciting!" he said. "But mine fell into place on Small World Day. I reconnected with so many of the kids I've known over the years... they're all grown up now, of course... and many of them invited me to come and see them... so, before the day was over, my calendar was full. Edna and I are going to tour the country, visiting them and meeting their spouses and children. That will keep me busy while I wait in breathless anticipation for your book to come out."

Everybody laughed. And they all asked for autographed copies.

As we prepared to say goodbye, Brie said it was too bad the Professor wasn't part of this.

I shook my head. "It's not his kind of party."

"He's a strange bird," Woody said. "But I've got to hand it to him. He came through."

L'Monjello glanced at Brie and told me, "We sent him a thank-you note."

Brie smiled back at him. "If it hadn't been for the Professor..."

Each of us could've finished the sentence differently. Then again, if it hadn't been for him, none of us would've been around to do so.

When the call ended, Maggie poked her head around my cubicle. "Fru's down in the lobby. He wants to come up."

"I'm not going to talk to him, Maggie. Stop asking."

My computer buzzed and another face appeared on the screen. This time it was the Professor.

He looked different somehow. More distinguished. More at peace with himself.

"Dak!" he said amicably. Then he added, "Do you mind if I call you 'Dak'?"

"Not at all," I told him. "Do you mind if I call you 'Professor'?"

He ignored the joke. He wanted to thank me for helping him find Basil.

Since Small World Day he had been busy re-establishing connections with colleagues and friends. It was difficult work—humbling, he said, but also gratifying. "I've misunderstood a lot of people over the years," he told me. "I'm trying to repair the damage as much as I can."

He had received a number of invitations to speak. "People want to hear the story," he said. "And I'm willing to tell them. But I'm no orator."

"You could've fooled me," I replied. "You were pretty eloquent at Estes Park."

"I can't take credit for that, Dak. And I think you know what I mean."

I understood. "Professor..." I paused a moment. "I want to ask you something, and I hope you won't take it the wrong way."

He looked surprised. "When have you ever worried about that?"

"I've started doing so," I told him. "Just recently."

"I know what you mean," he said. "I've been working on a few new things myself... like not taking offense so easily. What was your question?"

I paused again. "Did you honestly believe what you told us—that Basil was an alien?"

"Yes," he said. "He tried to tell me who he was right from the beginning. I couldn't accept it."

"But Vera knew better."

"Yes. She was an enigma. Everything she said was true, and yet the end result was a lie. I never misled any of you."

"Did you know she was right?"

"I had my suspicions. Remember when Mr. Parker asked me what galaxy Basil was from?"

"You couldn't answer him."

"Right, and that got me thinking, *Maybe Basil's been telling me the truth all along...*"

"It's strange that he relied on you anyway, even though you had the wrong idea about him."

"He works with us wherever we are, Dak. He doesn't wait for us to have him all figured out. We never will."

I pondered that a moment. "You've heard about The Kindred, I suppose?"

"Yes."

"And you know what that means..."

He nodded. "Basil didn't come to destroy the world after all. He came to save it."

"One thing I don't understand about that. He told us to find *him*. Why didn't he just warn us about The Kindred and leave it at that?"

"*They* weren't the problem, Dak. *We* are. Unless we get our hearts right toward one another, we'll always be in jeopardy. He knew that. He also knew we'd have to come together as a people to find him."

"That's one clever canine," I said. "So how does it make you feel? He chose you to get the ball rolling, after all."

He nodded. "And you." His eyes misted up. "Do you think our paths will cross again someday?"

"Well, Professor, you know what they say."

I paused for effect:

"It's a small world."

I waited, and the tiniest of smiles quivered at the corners of his lips.

"That was actually quite humorous," he said.

"I'm glad you noticed. There may be hope for you yet."

Just as we hung up, I heard a ding that made my heart skip a beat. Turning to page twenty of my digital *New York Times*, I found a message from Deep Throat.

She's alive, then! I thought.

"Tell Monica I appreciate what she tried to do, but I had to leave. I hope she understands."

There were many things I wanted to say to her, but I had no way of responding. Her message was Read-Only, as always. I imagined her texting me in her head, her one good eye rolling around like she was having a seizure.

"I'm heading out toward the stars," she continued. "Your Professor already tried the moon and that wasn't far enough. I'll just keep going until..."

My heart was racing. *You'll never outrun him, Vera.*

"I just can't face him. Monica has no idea what he's like. He expects too much of me."

I stared at the screen, waiting, but there was nothing more.

"Dak?"

I turned, startled. It was Maggie.

"You okay?"

I didn't know how to answer her. I looked back at the screen and read the message again. Was I trying to outrun him, too?

"He expects too much of me," she had said.

Oh yes, I would write the book, but I knew he wanted more than that. A lot more.

My dear Vera, it isn't just you. He expects too much of us all.

"Dak?"

I sighed. She wasn't going to let it go.

"Yes, Maggie, I'm okay."

It took me a minute to say the rest.

After another deep sigh, I added: "And you might as well tell Fru to come on up. I'm ready to see him now."

The End

ABOUT THE AUTHOR

Ronald R. Johnson has a PhD in Philosophy from Saint Louis University and teaches Philosophy and History at Spring Arbor University in Michigan (USA). He is the author of *Customer Service and the Imitation of Christ* and *What Does God Do from 9 to 5?* He lives with his wife Nancy and daughter Emily in Portage, Michigan.

65252745R00080

Made in the USA
Middletown, DE
24 February 2018